Thomas Buchanan Read

The wagoner of the Alleghanies

A poem of the days of seventy-six

Thomas Buchanan Read

The wagoner of the Alleghanies
A poem of the days of seventy-six

ISBN/EAN: 9783743335189

Manufactured in Europe, USA, Canada, Australia, Japa

Cover: Foto ©Andreas Hilbeck / pixelio.de

Manufactured and distributed by brebook publishing software (www.brebook.com)

Thomas Buchanan Read

The wagoner of the Alleghanies

THE

WAGONER OF THE ALLEGHANIES.

A POEM OF THE DAYS OF SEVENTY-SIX.

BY

THOMAS ~~BUCHANAN~~ READ.

"Thee,
Of the iron heart! they could not tame,
For thou wert of the mountains!"—BRYANT.

PHILADELPHIA:
J. B. LIPPINCOTT & CO.
1863.

DEDICATION.

TO JAMES L. CLAGHORN.

MIGHT I draw the inspiration
  Which the sky not oft awards,
And so join the constellation
  Of the death-defying bards;

Might I build some lofty moral,
  Reaching heavenward like a hill,
On whose top should grow the laurel,
  Leaning towards me at its will;—

I would gather all the honor
  Not to bind around my brow;
But to you, a grateful donor,
  I would come, as I do now,

3

And bring trophies, where the Ages
  Should behold our mingled names:
But, alas! these simple pages
  Are the most my labor claims.

Yet, should any leaves grow vernal
  In the summer-breath of praise,
Then for you, with hand fraternal,
  Let me twine my wreath of bays.

Rome, August 1, 1861.

ADVERTISEMENT.

THE scenes of this poem are chiefly laid on the banks of the Schuylkill, between Philadelphia and Valley Forge; the time, somewhat previous to and during a great part of the war of Independence.

CONTENTS.

10   CONTENTS.

PART III.

Look on your country, God's appointed stage,

Where man's vast mind its boundless course shall run:

For that it was your stormy coast He spread,—

A fear in winter; girdled you about

With granite hills, and made you firm and dread.

Let him who fears before the foeman shout,

Or gives one inch before a vein has bled,

Turn on himself and let the traitor out.

BOKER.

INTRODUCTION.

A GUEST was I at Berkley Hall,—
  And more behooves not guest to say:
The very pictures on the wall
  With kindness seemed to whisper, "Stay !"—
Old portraits of a dwindled line,
  From Lely's ruff and doublet down
  To Copley's matchless coat and gown,
Or Stuart's later touch divine.
Still from their frames of gold or oak,
  A knight or lady shepherdess,
  In valor or in loveliness,
Leaned through the twilight air and spoke:
They whispered that the road was dark,
  And lone the highway by the river,
That past recall the latest bark
Had swept the landing of the park,—

There on the stream I still might mark
　Its fading path of ripples quiver,
And hear the shore-wave running after,
Like childhood with a voice of laughter.

'Twas evening, and the autumn fire
Was feasting at the well-built pyre,
Where every log, with glowing mirth,
Poured from its breast of ample girth
Some memory of April birth,
　To cheer the hearthstone of October.
There, conscious of his place and worth,
　One lordly hound, with visage sober,
Sheathed his large eyes in sleep's eclipse,
　While visions of the woodland chase
　Disturbed the slumber on his face
With twinklings at his ears and lips.

That honored hearth was like a gate
　Wide with the welcome of old days;
No sulphur-fuming, modern grate,
Which black bitumen daily crams,
But waved between its ample jambs
　Its flag of hospitable blaze.
A century gone 'twas lined with tiles,
　Like those the hearths of Holland show;

And still each Scripture picture smiles
And brightens in the hickory glow.

Oft from those painted sermons rude,
In musing hours of solitude,
A voiceless thought hath searched the heart
Beyond the theologian's art.
A moral winged with verse may reach
A soul no weightier words will teach,
As arrow from the archer's bow
Has cleaved where falchion failed to go;
And truths from out a picture oft,
In colors as the iris soft,
May shed an influence to remain
Where argument would strive in vain.

The chairs were quaint, antique, and tall,
As in some old baronial hall;
And in an alcove dusk and dim,
    Like Denmark's mailed and phantom king,
A suit of armor tall and grim
    With upraised glaive seemed beckoning.
And had it walked, the gazer, drawn,
Must needs have followed on and on!
The perforated steel confessed
What death had pierced the wearer's breast.

Near by, upon a throne upreared,
A harp of bygone times appeared:
The graceful form was deftly made,
With pearl and precious woods inlaid;
And in the firelight, as of old,
It flushed the shadowy niche with gold.

In all the orchestras which lift
    The soul with rapture caught from far,
    As in a bright triumphal car
Round which celestial splendors shift,
No instrument of earth affords
    An influence so divine and deep,
    As when the flying fingers sweep
The harp, with all its wondrous chords.
Around its honored form there lives
    Romance mysterious, vague, and old:
I see the shapes which history gives
    The bards in dim traditions told,—
With visions of great kingly halls,
Where red, barbaric splendor falls;
But chiefly I behold and hear—
While bends a troop of seraphs near—
    The angels, with their locks of gold.

Such shadowy halls of deep repose
A New-World homestead seldom shows;
But such the traveller frequent sees,
Embowered within ancestral trees,
In that maternal isle whose breast
    First warmed our eagle into life,
    And then, with rude, unnatural strife,
Pushed the brave offspring from her nest,—
    Which, launched upon its sunward track,
    No voice on earth could summon back.

Here, while I slowly paced the room,
Strange visions filled the fitful gloom.
On soft, invisible feet they came;
I heard them speak,—or was't the flame
That muttered in the chimney wide?
Faint shadows wavered at my side,
My spirit heard a spirit sigh,
While gauzy garments rustled by!
A pallid phantom of the fire
Leapt o'er the high flame wildly higher,—
A blaze that vanished with a bound!
A whine escaped the sleeping hound,—
A sudden wind swept up the lane,
    And drove the leaves like frighted herds;

2*

Some, like the ghosts of summer-birds,
Fluttered against the window-pane.

Hawthorne, my friend, had I your wand,
How, at the waving of my hand,
The place, and all its grandeur gone,
Should on the marvelling vision dawn!
Each shepherdess, or warrior bold,
    Each knight and dame, in ruff and frill,
    Obedient to the wizard will,
Should step from antique oak or gold;
Bright eyes should glance, sweet voices sing,
    And light feet trip the waxen floor;
And round the festive board should ring
    The friendly goblets, as of yore;
And Love's sweet grief be newly told
Under the elm-trees, as of old.
But, ah! the hazel wand you wield
    Was grown by that enchanted stream
    Which sometimes flashes through my dream,
But flows not through my barren field!

The host came in: he took my hand:
    He saw the wonder on my face,
And said, "Ah, yes: I understand:
    You marvel at this curious place,

Which starts your fancy into play.
My locks, you see, are somewhat gray :
　What touches you on me is lost.
This white hair drives romance away,
　As flowers are driven by the frost.
But if a tale would please your ear,
There's one which you are free to hear.

Within a little, secret drawer
Of this black, antique escritoir,
I found a simple golden case,
Which held the semblance of a face
So wondrous in its wild attire
　Of floating robe and flying hair,
　And eyes that thrilled the very air
To pleasure with their starry fire,
That instantly the long-passed name
Blazed on my memory like a flame ;
　And old traditions, dimmed by years,
Breathed from invisible lips there came,
　And lingered in my credulous ears,
And night and day disturbed my soul,
Until, perforce, I wrote the whole :
That is the picture,—this the scroll.

Draw near; and let wild Autumn blow:
He does but fan the lighted pyre:
Between the warmth of wine and fire
Perchance the verse may thaw and flow
From off the visionary lyre
As in the days of long ago.

PART I.

I.

BERKLEY'S BRIDE.

My grandsire, when he built the place,
  Sir Hugh, (you may behold him there,
  With ruffles, cue, and powdered hair,
And proper blandness on his face,)
Was Tory, and his loyal soul
  No rebel dream could e'er beguile:
He would have had the land in whole,
Colossal, touching either pole,
  A likeness of his native isle!
Hence the Elizabethan gables,
The lawns, the elms, the antique stables,
And all this lumber called *virtu*,
This old time frowning down the new.

But, ere I tell you more of him,
  Or point the objects strange and quaint,

23

I pray you note these figures dim,
  Half hid in dust and cracking paint.
That picture of those little ones,
Which represent Alcmena's sons,
Young Hercules and his weaker brother,—
  One with the snake in his baby hands,
  Crushing it as in iron bands,
While in affright recoils the other,—
Are portraits which the Berkley mother,
In all the wealth of parental joys,
Had painted of her two fair boys;
And pictured thus, because she knew
There was that difference 'twixt the two.
  The child who holds the writhing snake
  Was Ralph; the one who seems to quake
And shudder back,—that was Sir Hugh.

They grew, and oft the quarrel loud
  Raged 'twixt them when they were together:
Sir Hugh was sullen, wintry, proud,
  The other fierce as mad March weather,—
A swift, cloud-blowing, whirling day,
That o'er all obstacles makes way,
Whether in wrath or whether in play,
Striding on to the stormy end,
Breaking what will not bow or bend.

The soul which lights that face of paint,
You well discern, would scorn restraint;
And when he grew a stripling tall,
  Knowing himself the younger brother,
  And feeling the coldness of the other,
The place for him proved far too small:
So, staying not for leave to ask,
Our Hercules went to seek his task;
And, lest his family might reclaim
Their truant, took another name,
Joining the army.   Tradition tells
He did some daring miracles.
'Twas said he fell in a midnight trench
At Fort du Quesne, against the French.
Sir Hugh was then the only son
To hand the name of Berkley on.

His lady—she who bears a crook,
  And shepherds at her careful side
A lamb, while from her eyes a look
  Of mildness chastens half her pride—
Gave to the house one child, and died.

That child a maiden grown you see,
With laughing eyes and tresses free,
  Which wellnigh mocked the painter's skill:

3

It glows as if some morning beam
Had poured here in a golden stream,
  And, when the sun passed, lingered still.

A year or two went by, and then
  His heart was vacant as his hall.
  No pleasure answered to his call,
No joy was in the world of men :
One passion only swayed his mind,
  And thrust all other thoughts aside,—
  The passion of ancestral pride.
The blindest of all eyes most blind
Are those forever turned behind.
Sheer to the past he held his face,
  Like some mad boatman on a river,
With eyes still on some long-gone place,
  Until he feels the shock and shiver
  Which tells him he is gone forever.

The empty hall, or vacant heart,
  When a new-comer passes in,
Throwing the dusty doors apart,
  Sounds and re-echoes with a din
Which makes the ghostly shadows start
  And fly into the dusk remote ;
  The webs about the casements float,

And flutter on the sudden gust;
The sun pours in its golden dust;
　　The phantom Silence dies in air,
And rapidly from hall to hall,
　　With questioning eyes and backward hair,
　　Wild Wonder speeds, and mounts the stair,
Chasing the echoes' far footfall.

Thus into Berkley's hall and heart,
　　Led by his fancy's sudden whim,
Passed a new bride,—a face to dart
　　Strange lustre through the twilight dim,—
　　A soul that even startled him,
Until he half forgot his pride:
　　Else had he never stooped to embower
　　Beneath his ancient roof the flower
To common wildwood vines allied.

Thus oft the passion most profound,
　　Which triumphed over all the past,
With unexpected halt, wheels round,
　　And contradicts itself at last.

He took her from a rival's breast.
The hot youth dared him to the test:

Alas! he fell on Berkley's steel;
And, it is said, through woe or weal
She ever loved the rival best.

Her heart was like a crystal spring,
Fluttered by every breezy wing:
Was there a cloud? a darker shade
Was in its deep recesses laid;
Was there a sun? the pool, o'errun
With glory, seemed to mock the sun.
Her black hair, oft with violets twined,
(Her heart was with the wildest flowers,)
Tossed back at random, wooed the wind,
That chased her through the forest bowers.
The woodman felt his hand relax
A moment on the lifted axe,
As through the vistas of the trees
He saw her glide, a spirit blithe;
Or, when she tript the harvest leas,
The singing mower stayed his scythe,
Watched where she fled, then took his way,
And, mowing, sang no more that day.

With no misgiving thought or doubt,
Her fond arms clasped his child about,

In the full mantle of her love;
 For whoso loves the darling flowers
 Must love the bloom of human bowers,—
The types of brightest things above.
One day—one happy summer-day—
 She prest it to her tender breast:
The sunshine of its head there lay
 As pillowed in its native rest,—
A blissful picture of repose,
A lily bosomed on a rose:
The smallest lily of the vale
Making the rose's sweet breast pale.

One only day,—and then the sire,
 Still to his former spirit true,
 Lest the young bud should take the hue
Of that which glowed too fondly by her,—
Of that sweet wildling, nature's own,—
And thereby learn the look and tone
Of spirits alien unto pride,
Conveyed her to the river's side.—
 For months his household felt eclipse,—
 And one of his own many ships
Bore her across the ocean wide;
And soon in her ancestral isle
Was shed the sunshine of her smile.

3*

Ere half the summer passed away,
The lady Berkley grew less gay,
And, like a captured forest-fawn,
She seemed to mourn some freedom gone,—
Mourned for her native mountain-wild,
From which her feet had been beguiled.

Her cheeks grew pale, and dim her eye,
    Her voice was low, her mirth was stayed;
Upon her heart there seemed to lie
    The darkness of a nameless shade;
She paced the house from room to room,
Her form became a walking gloom.

The menials, in their fancy wise,
    Glared at each other with strange leers;
And, when she met her husband's eyes,
    Her sad soul burst to instant tears.
He wondered with a cold surmise,
    And questioned with as heartless words:
And could it be a woodland flower
Would pine within such stately bower?
    Or, favored o'er all forest birds,
Could this one droop with strange desires
Within a cage of golden wires?

Have you beheld a mountain-brook
Turned to some cultured garden-nook,—
  How it grows stagnant in the pool,
  Like some wild urchin in a school
That saddens o'er a hateful book?
Thus grew the lady, and her look
  Became at last as one insane:
  The cloud that long o'ercast her brain
  Still whirled with gusty falls of rain,
Which drowned her heart and dimmed her eyes,
As when the dull àutumnal skies
  Long blur the dreary window-pane.

One morn, strange wonder filled the place,
  And fruitless searching filled the day;
The stream, the woodland, gave no trace:
  They only knew she passed away,—
Passed like a vision in the air,
With naught to tell of how or where.

Tradition adds how, night by night,
With hanging hair and robes of white,
With pallid hands together prest
In pain upon her aching breast,
Her spirit walked from room to room,
  As if in search of something lost;

That even Berkley shunned the gloom,
　　Fearing to meet that breathless ghost;
For some averred her form had been
Afloat upon the river seen;
While some, with stouter words, replied,
The maniac lady wandered wide
Upon her native mountain-side.

II.

THE WILD WAGONER.

In days long gone, "The Ship and Sheaf"
Was deemed of goodly inns the chief:—
"The Ship,"—because its ample door
Fronted the barks that lined the shore,
  Where oft the sun, o'er Delaware,
Looking 'twixt masts and cordage bare,
Their shadows threw on the sanded floor,
  Sailing a phantom vessel there.

And there the crews from far-off climes
Reeled in and sang their rough sea-rhymes,
With laughter learned from the ocean gale,
As clinked their dripping cups of ale;
While froth was dashed o'er many a lip,
Like foam against a speeding ship,

And tables chronicled in scars
The tankards and the thirsty tars.

" The Sheaf,"—because the wagoner there,
    The captain of the highway-ship,
Fresh breathing of his mountain air,
    Hung on the wall his coat and whip;
And farmer, bringing his stores to town,
And drover, who drove his cattle down,
    Conversed of pastures and of sheaves,
The season's drouth, or ruinous rain,
Or told of fabulous crops of grain,
    Or fields where grazed incredible beeves.

'Twas April, and the evening winds
Were rattling at the open blinds;
The sign, upon its hinge of rust,
Made dreary answer to the gust,
That smote the masts like an ocean squall,
And, whistling, mocked the boatswain's call.

The latch went up; the door was thrown
Awide, as by a tempest blown;
While, bold as an embodied storm,
Strode in a dark and stalwart form,

And all the lights in the sudden wind
Flared as he slammed the door behind.

The noisy revellers ceased their din,
   And into the corner skulked the cur,
As the startled keeper welcomed in
   The feared and famous wagoner!
Not long they brooked the keen eye-glance
Who gazed into that countenance;
And even in his mildest mood
His voice was sudden, loud, and rude
As is a swollen mountain-stream.
He spoke as to a restive team.
His team was of the wildest breed
   That ever tested wagoner's skill:
Each was a fierce, unbroken steed,
   Curbed only by his giant will;
And every ostler quaked with fear
What time his loud bells wrangled near.

On many a dangerous mountain-track,
While oft the tempest burst its wrack,
When lightning, like his mad whip-lash,
Whirled round the team its crooked flash,
   And horses reared in fiery fright,

While near them burst the thunder-crash,
    Then heard the gale his voice of might.
The peasant from his window gazed,
    And, staring through the darkened air,
Saw, when the sudden lightning blazed,
    The fearful vision plunging there!

And oft on many a wintry hill
    He dashed from out the vale below,
    And heaved his way through drifts of snow,
While all his wheels, with voices shrill,
    Shrieked to the frosty air afar,
    As if December's tempest-car
Obeyed the winter's maniac will.

Ye knew him well, ye mountain-miles,
Throughout your numerous dark defiles:—
Where Juniata leaps away
On feathery wings of foam and spray;
Or queenly Susquehanna smiles,
Proud in the grace of her thousand isles;
Where Poet and Historian fling
Their light o'er classic Wyoming;
And you, ye green Lancastrian fields,
Rich with the wealth which Ceres yields;

And Chester's storied vales and hills,
  In depths of rural calm divine,
  Where reels the flashing Brandywine,
And dallies with its hundred mills.

Such was the figure, strange and wild;
And at his side a twelve-years child—
An eagle-eyed, bright, wondering lad,
In rustic winter garments clad—
Entered, and held the wagoner's hand,
While on his visage, flushed and tanned,
A pleasure mingled with amaze
Parted his lips and filled his gaze.
His hair was wavy, long, and black,
And from his forehead drifted back
By the last greeting of the gale,
Where still the random rain and hail
Clung glistening like the tangled pearls
In careless locks of Indian girls.

The host with usual "welcome" smiled,
And praised the bright-eyed stranger child;
Whereat the wagoner lightly spake:—
" Be all your praising for his sake:
I found him in the wagon-trough
  A-swinging like a cradled thing;

4

With angry words I bade him off,—
  He stared with large eyes wondering,
And answered that his way was long,
  His knees were tired, his feet were sore;
  And then his face new brightness wore,
And straight his spirit burst to song:
  I listened, and my frown gave o'er.

My nature, like my hand, is rough,
My heart is of rude mountain stuff;
And yet, I own, a laughing child
Can make at times my temper mild.

I placed him on the wheel-horse back,
  Where shoulder-shaken bells were ringing.
The king of all the bells was he,—
So silver-clear his voice of glee;
  And there he cheered the way with singing,
Till music filled our dreary track.

There is not much I ask or need;
Yet would I give my favorite steed
To sing the song he sang to-day,
And for a heart as light and gay:
The very team went rearing mad
With joy beneath his voice so glad,

As when the steeds of battle hear
The wild war-clarion ringing near.
Come, my young wood-bird, sing again
That breezy song,—that mountain-strain."
And thus, from lips of fresh delight,
The wild and artless song took flight.

SONG.

Where sweeps round the mountains
   The cloud on the gale,
And streams from their fountains
   Leap into the vale,—
Like frighted deer leap when
   The storm with his pack
Rides over the steep in
   The wild torrent's track,—
Even there my free home is;
   There watch I the flocks
Wander white as the foam is
   On stairways of rocks.
Secure in the gorge there
   In freedom we sing,
And laugh at King George, where
   The Eagle is king.

II.

I mount the wild horse with
  No saddle or rein,
And guide his swift course with
  A grasp on his mane;
Through paths steep and narrow,
  And scorning the crag,
I chase with my arrow
  The flight of the stag.
Through snow-drifts engulfing,
  I follow the bear,
And face the gaunt wolf when
  He snarls in his lair,
And watch through the gorge there
  The red panther spring,
And laugh at King George, where
  The Eagle is king.

III.

When April is sounding
  His horn o'er the hills,
And brooklets are bounding
  In joy to the mills,—
When warm August slumbers
  Among her green leaves,

And Harvest encumbers
  Her garners with sheaves,—
When the flail of November
  Is swinging with might,
And the miller December
  Is mantled with white,—
In field and in forge there
  The free-hearted sing,
And laugh at King George, where
  The Eagle is king.

Some praised the voice, and some, in doubt,
With look uncertain, gazed about;
And some, with loyal feeling strong,
Condemned the singer and the song,
And swore it was a rebel strain
They would not calmly hear again.
Whereat the wagoner's eyes of fire
Flashed round a withering look of ire;
His brows grew black, his temple-veins
Grew large, like brooks with sudden rains;
From face to face he bent his glance,
And searched each quailing countenance.

Thus for a time great Henry stood,
When cries of " treason" fired his blood,

Till from his quivering lips was hurled
The answer that awoke the world.
And thus the last of all that band,*
The giants of our native land,
The safeguards in our darkest hours,
Our bulwarks and our sentinel towers,
Oft stood, and from his cavernous eyes
Sped to the heart his great replies:
Far in advance he fiercely sent
The fiery shaft of argument;
And, when he spoke, 'twas but to tell
In thunder where the red bolt fell!

Thus stood the wagoner, till at length,
With voice subdued to conscious strength,
He spoke, and said, "Our eagle's wing
Shall mount, the eagle *shall* be king!
And jackals shall be heard no more
When Freedom's monarch bird shall soar."

'Twas passed, and none essayed reply;
Defeat or triumph filled each eye.
Whence came the boy? was asked in vain;
　What errand brought the truant down?

---

* Webster.

What would he in the noisy town?—
Conjecture but replied again.

The wagoner drew the host aside,
    And said, "The storm approaches near,
And soon its bolts must be defied:
    For me its thunders bring no fear;
    But for this tender fledgling here,
'Twere well if he a while might rest
Secure in some protected nest.

This hand that long has grasped the whip
Must shortly take within its grip
Another scourge, and boldly deal
The blow a tyrant needs must feel:
Hence it were best the boy should be
Removed a little space from me,
Lest that the battling oak might wrong
The eaglet it has sheltered long."

Then said the landlord, as he took
    Another survey of the face,
    "It was no fancy made me trace
In that young form the Ringbolt look.
Although your answer seemed to say
He crossed but now your townward way."

" Even as I told," the wagoner said
" The urchin, wild of heart and head,
Wishing to follow where I led,
Stealthily stole behind the wain,
Breasting the gusts of hail and rain.
It was no easy task, I fear,
For one so young to keep so near.
For miles I thought I heard the beat
And splash, behind, of following feet.
You well may guess with what surprise
I met the truant's laughing eyes,
And how that face of brave delight,
While in the trough he sat upright,
Put all my chiding words to flight.

All day my thoughts were somewhat sad
With too much dwelling on the lad,
Contriving where I best might trust
His sheltered head when comes the gust.
For when it comes, I must be where
The thickest dangers are to dare ;
And there are cowards who would make
The boy a victim for my sake.
It was for this I would not own
Before these Tories of the town
     The child was aught to me beside

A friendless truant wandering down,
    Whom, pitying, I allowed to ride.

And now, my friend, I ask of you
    To aid me in my urgent need,—
To give or find the boy a home
Where present danger may not come:
For this you shall receive your due,
    Even though it cost my last good steed."

The host replied, "Leave that to me:
    There's many a one comes here to dine
Would joy beside his chair to see
    So lithe an urchin serve his wine."

"Scrve!"—but between the wagoner's teeth
The word was crushed to instant death:
His brow grew black a moment, then
As quickly it was cleared again.
" Be it, good landlord, as you say,"
He murmured: " 'tis but for a day,"
And then abruptly turned away.

Under the gable-roof the boy
Soon prest the soothing bed with joy:

A little while he heard the sigh
Of winds like spirits hovering nigh,
The weather-vane that creaked aloof,
The slumberous rain along the roof,
   And breathed the scent of bundled herbs
Close to the waspy rafters hung;
Then heard the hour from the belfry flung,
   And then the watch along the curbs,
   With voice that warns but not disturbs;
Then slept, and dreamed of his native place,
And woke with the red sun on his face.

THE HEIRESS.

OUT of the sea, and over the land,
Over the level Jersey sand,
Making the bay with splendor quiver,
Flashing a glory up the river,
Came the morn on its wheel of fire,
Flinging flame from its glowing tire.

And with the morning, up the tide,
Through golden vapor dim descried,
A distant ship was seen to ride,
Vague as a vessel in a dream,—
More in the sky than on the stream.

Down to the wharf a horseman rode,
As oft on many a morn before,

47

To note the barks that inland bore;
And when his glance had swept the shore,
His face with sudden pleasure glowed.
He gave the rein to a boy near by,
And raised him in his stirrups high,
And poised the glass at his anxious eye.—
Long time with breathless breast he gazed,
Then deeply sighed, "Now, Heaven be praised!"
And to a skipper sauntering past
　　He cried, "Unless my vision fail,
　　I know the set of yonder sail
And the streamer at her mast!"
The skipper then a moment scanned
The ship beneath his shading hand,
　　And answered, with a sudden smile,
"Ay, ay, sir: I should know that deck:
The same that saved us once from wreck,—
　　'The Lady of the Isle!'"

In haste the rider grasped the rein,
And turned his restive steed again,
Yet, ere he sped, with hand of joy
A coin of silver flung the boy,
And, as he threw, looked down and smiled;
　　And then, as if some form had risen

To meet him from its churchyard prison,
He stared upon the wondering child.

He would have spoke; but gayly now,
Before the startled words could join,
The boy was toying with the coin,
Twirling it in the sunny air,
Laughing to see it flashing there.

A moment the rider pressed his brow,
Then dashed the vision in scorn aside,
And glanced again o'er the distant tide,
And, with a face of new delight,
Struck to the rowels the glittering spurs:
The steed obeyed the urging burrs,
And bore proud Berkley out of sight.

The hour went by.   Before the town
The ship came up; the sails were doft;
The happy crew, alow and aloft,
Sang as the anchor rattled down,—
Down and down, as the windlass flew,
Linking the Old World with the New.

A crowd was gathering on the wharf,
A crowd leaned on the vessel's side,
And here and there a waving scarf
Bespoke some welcome friend descried.

5

At the open gang a maiden stood,
Reflected in the happy flood,—
Oh, enviable flood, how blest
With such a vision on thy breast!—
Stood like a timid, startled fawn
Gazing where its mates are gone;
Stood like a white star in the dawn,
Looking with inquiring eyes
Where its westward pathway lies.

Loud rumbling to the shore anon
A stately coach came proudly drawn,
With the ancient Berkley arms thereon;
And soon to land the maid, whose hair
Shed amber beauty in the air,
Was borne, and on her father's breast
The long-expected child was prest.

The gold of fifteen summer suns
    Was tangled in young Esther's locks;
Her voice, it was a rill that runs
    Half spray among the flowers and rocks;
The hues of the dewiest violet
Within her liquid eyes were set;
Her form was small, her figure light,
As is some fabled fountain-sprite;

The aerial scarf about her twined
Like gossamer, seemed to woo the wind;
A shape so light, she seemed to be
That vision which poets only see,—
The spirit of that iris small
Poised on the mist of a waterfall.

Foremost amid the crowd amazed
The truant urchin stood and gazed.
His sunbrown cheek and large dark eyes,
His long black hair and rustic guise,
Contrasted with the maiden bright,
In her auroral beauty dight,
As if some offspring of the eve
His dusk home in the west should leave,
To gaze, by love and wonder drawn,
On some fair daughter of the dawn.

Again the proud man, in his joy,
Shuddered as he beheld the boy;
But the happy maid looked round and smiled,—
Smiled through her tears at the vision wild
Of flashing eyes and raven hair,
And cheeks long tanned by mountain-air.
That smile went to the urchin's heart,
Secure as ever archer's dart

Sped to the target's central shade,
Long quivering where it struck and stayed.

But soon the carriage, with rumbling loud,
Conveyed the lovely shape from sight;
And he felt like a traveller in the night
When the moon glides into a thunder-cloud
And will no more return to sight.

Out of the vessel came many a box
Of Berkley's treasures manifold;
Some with iron bands and locks,
Some from the cabin, some from the hold.
Some were carried, some were rolled;
But one, with curious shape, to shore
With careful hands the sailors bore:
They said it contained a harp of gold
Of strange device,—they knew no more.

A wain took up the various load;
The truant followed it out of town,
By wild, adventurous wonder drawn
Along the winding highway road,
Where Berkley Hall looked proudly down
Over its river-reaching lawn.

When Berkley saw the boy again,
    He took him by the willing hand,
And asked him questions simple, plain,
    In easy words to understand;
But still the youth, with laughing eyes,
Made answer with wide, vague replies;
Nor would he tell from whence he came,
But answered; "Ugo" was his name.

And then the master smoothed his hair,
    And said, in soothing accents mild,
    "It is a barren world, my child,
And full of hearts as bleak and bare
    As is a winter heath forlorn,
    Where only thrives the tangled thorn;
And when a stray lamb wanders there
    Its sides are sorely fleeced and torn.
What can you to secure your bread?
Or how at night procure your bed?"

The boy looked up with wondering face,
Which told such thought had never place
Within the precincts of his brain;
And then he gayly cried again,
With voice on laughter's sudden wing,
"So please you, master, I can sing!"
                    5*

" A fair profession, by my troth !"
Sir Hugh replied, " when tune and words
Are fitted well, and, suiting both,
The spirit with the voice accords :
But they come off the hungriest birds
Who, so enamored of their strain,
Sing while the others, in the grain,
With voiceless but industrious beaks,
Feed well through all the harvest weeks.
But pour me from your frolic heart
A sample of your vocal art."

His simple tongue no urging stayed,
And thus the call for song was paid.

S O N G.

I.

Where the peaks first greet the morn,
Where the mighty streams are born,—
Streams that sweep from east to west,
Bearing great arks on their breast,—
Where the eagle rears her young
Barren rocks and pines among,
There's a child which knows no fear,
In the home of the mountaineer.

II.

Oft among the forests wild
The lone woodman hears the child
Singing with the earliest dawn,
And his playmate is a fawn:
When that fawn's broad antlers spring,
They shall hear him louder sing;
Then his startling song shall cheer
Far and wide the mountaineer.

III.

Then his hero-hand shall take
In its grasp a crested snake,
And its front, so proudly crowned,
Shall be humbled to the ground,—
Humbled, trampled in the sand,—
And no longer fright the land;
Then the world shall thrill to hear
Songs of that young mountaineer.

The listener, halfway frowning, smiled,
And said, "Perchance you are that child
Far wandering from your mountains wild,
And full of those obnoxious songs
But fit for rebel ears and tongues?"

"Oh, no!" the laughing youth replied:
" Although I come from the mountain-side,
My songs I learned from a schoolman gray,
Who, when the children went to play,
Oft called us round him in a ring,
And, singing, taught us all to sing."

Then Berkley's brow relaxed his frown,
And he looked still more kindly down;
For there was something in that voice
Which made him sigh and yet rejoice;
And then he cried, "Come in! come in!—
I care not what your kith or kin,
Your face and singing please me well;
And, if you will, here may you dwell,
And be, till your maturer age,
A gentle lady's faithful page."

IV.

THE WELCOME.

DAYS past; and now from Berkley Hall,
　　When evening sped her herald star,
Gay music, with wild rise and fall,
Streamed on the air; the windows all　　.
　　Shot their red beams of splendor far,
Firing the dark like beacon-torches;
　　While, like a wedding-train, there flowed
　　Gay coaches up the winding road,
Grating the gravel near the porches.

Form after form, in rich attire
　　Of gems and rustling garments bright,
　　Swept like shadows out of the night
　　Into the sudden blaze of light,
Gleaming as in a robe of fire.

The peasant on the distant slope,
Agaze at joys beyond his hope,
Believing the world was what it seemed,—
  Alas that others should be more wise!—
Beheld them glide, as he fondly deemed,
  Into a transient paradise.
Along the casements he saw them pass,
As phantoms on the flaming glass;
And when the music awoke the dance,
Like shadows they seemed to sway and glance,
Or revellers seen in a dreamer's trance.

Fond soul, could some kind sprite have shown
  Some hearts beneath those robes and gems,
The smile without, within the groan,
He had not sighed that, poor, unknown,
He stood apart in the open air,
Or bartered his peace with the proudest there
  To wear the wealth of diadems.
On the side of the neighboring height
He saw the modest cottage light
Gleam, like a glow-worm in the night,
  Through the foliage deep and dark:
Strange contrast to the splendor bright
  Burning in midst of Berkley Park.

And could the marvelling man have seen
As clearly into that home serene
As into that glittering hall of pride,—
　　Have seen the pastor's patriarch hair
Bending over the volume wide,
　　And heard the old clock on the stair
　　Saying its "Amen" to the prayer,
And, when the evening hymn was sung,
Joining with its silver tongue,—
He had not sighed o'er his station mean,
　　While hearkening to that worldly din,
　　Nor envied the tinsel triumph thin
Of the stateliest hero of the scene.
But hearts are human moths, alas!
Fluttering against the glittering glass,
Flying from Nature's flowery ways
To worship and die at a transient blaze.

Within, beneath the chandeliers,
Wealth, envious of her two compeers,
Beauty and Wit, her shoulders bare,
Strode with her diamond front in air.

There Beauty walked, too oft a shell,
A bower of roses round a cell,

A casket exquisitely bright,
With not a jewel hid from sight;
Like those proud piles by travellers found
In foreign lands, with statues crowned,
Covered with all that charms the eye,
While within sits Poverty,
Cowering in the ancestral dust,
With scarce an ember or a crust.

And Wit, with sparkling glance, was there,
With flashing words of transient glare,
Of satire or of flattery,—
Thoughts that lorded or bowed the knee:
They who lord it with haughtiest brow
Have ever the supplest knees to bow.
All these, Wealth, Beauty, Wit, bright three,—
    Graces they were by Heaven designed,
But oftener grow, through vanity,
    The vices that ensnare the mind.

But there was one in whom these three
Were joined in sweetest unity,—
To all the Virtues reconciled,
But chiefly Charity's favorite child.
    So bright the spirit her form enshrined,
    So clearly the face displayed the mind,

That the coldest gazer's heart 'gan melt,
And, in after-days of memory, felt
    A kindlier impulse toward his kind:
And it was all to welcome her
The glittering groups collected were.

Through the crowd, on her father's arm,—
    How proud he was! how very proud!—
She passed, like a ray of sunshine warm
    Cleaving its way through a broken cloud.

First there was silence,—breaths long drawn,
    As they would breathe her beauty in,
    And eyes full-orbed, as they would win
New light from her enchanted dawn;
And then the sudden whisper stirred,
Like winds within the aspens heard.
The proud man caught the applause around,
That thrilled his depths of pride profound,
Where it echoed, like a bugle wound
Near caverns that prolong the sound.

Then to her thronéd harp he led,
Where lustre of gold and pearl was shed,
    Like the light that flushed the air
    Around the maiden's pearl-looped hair.

6

A moment her timorous fingers tried
The chords that tremorously replied,
Like reeds beside a little lake
Warned by a breeze ere the winds awake:
She toyed with the prelude; but not long
The herald notes foreran the song.

SONG.

I.

What though my feet have wandered far
　　Through groves and lawns of antique shores,
Where ever to the morning star
　　The enamored lark her love-song pours,
And through enchanted woods and vales
　　Romance still walks, a spirit free,
Thrilled by the poet-nightingales:
　　I turn, dear native land, to thee.

II.

It is not that thy giant floods
　　Sweep seaward with unrivalled flow;
It is not that thy pathless woods
　　Have majesty no others show;
Not for thy matchless inland seas,
　　Wider than eagle's eye discerns,

Nor mountains vast;—'tis not for these
  My heart, dear land, to thee returns:—

III.

Not for thy seasons, though they sweep
  From unknown continents of ice,
Or, waked in tropic forests deep,
  Bring summer from the land of spice;
Not that thy fiery forest-trees,
  At harvest-close, with splendors burn
In hues triumphant;—not for these
  To thee, dear land, my steps return.—

IV.

Not only that my native hearth
  Is shrined among thy greenest hills,
Or that my earliest infant mirth
  Was learned among thy flowers and rills,
But, chiefly, that before thee opes
  A glorious future, grand and free,
And thou hast all my brightest hopes,—
  For this, dear land, I turn to thee.

To give the words by a maiden sung
After they have passed her tongue,

When more than half of all the grace
Was in her voice and on her face,
Is but to render a cup long drawn,
With all its effervescence gone;
'Tis but to treasure in after-hours
The garland of faded and dewless flowers
That in the flood of the banquet-light
Made the wearer's brow more bright.
Had another dared the same to sing,
They had denounced it a rebel thing;
But from her lips could come no wrong:
So they praised the singer and the song.

Mid those who listened, too rapt to praise,
Like blossoms that close in the sun's full blaze,
Folding the ecstasy into the heart
In silence, lest the smallest part
Should exhale on the breath of joy exprest,
Stood one, a chance-invited guest,
Half hidden by a curtain's fold,
Too modest and proud to be more bold,
A youth—the neighboring pastor's son—
Whose mind and mien had already won
The wide applause which oft exalts
Till envy finds the virtues faults.

A student he was, with cheeks grown pale,
Long bleached in that scholastic vale
Where mild-eyed Meditation camps
Among her midnight books and lamps.

But as he stood and heard her sing,
 And gazed with charméd lips apart,
 The joy long nestling in his heart
Flew to his cheek on flaming wing.
So feels the prisoner when his cell
Flies open, as by a miracle;
So glows he, breathing what freedom yields
That first hour in the summer fields.

Yes; love, and wonder, and delight,
All three into his breast took flight;
And those who knew young Edgar best
Noted the change on his face confessed.

Near by, with scarlet coat and plume,
Like a bonfire in the room,
An officer of the royal troops
Blazed among the admiring groups,
Who, when his eye approval glanced,
 Or when he spoke the applauding word,
Deemed Berkley's honor was advanced;

And he, too, felt a new delight,
And deigned from his great warrior height
　　To stoop, and own his heart was stirred.

Outside, in the stars' still light,
Like a spirit of the night,
Pressing close to the window-pane,
With eyes of wonder and mirth insane,
There looked a face which shunned the gaze,
Coming and going, as a shadow plays
When the wind, with rise and fall,
Sways the elm-shade on the wall.

This with a smile the maiden saw,
Saw it come and then withdraw ;
　　And oft they knew not why she smiled,
　　Nor saw the vision strange and wild
Which she beheld with looks of joy,—
The frolic-hearted truant boy.
　　Thus oft beside a delirious child
The watchers see upon its face
Expressions which they cannot trace,
And where its eyes so fondly turn
They look, but nothing can discern,
Still conscious of a presence near
Of what they cannot see or hear.

After the supper and the wine,
Where flowed the Moselle and the Rhine,
And Burgundy and prouder Spain,
Disputing, held divided reign,—
For Berkley deemed the worst of faults
Poor brands, or scant-provided vaults,—
Out they sallied into the air;
And the great white moon was there.
In merry groups about the green
They strolled, and praised the night serene;
Here the laugh and there the song
Waked from sleep the feathery throng,
Nested in the vernal realms
Of the poplars and the elms.
Their heads unsheathing from the wing,
  Some, which only the dark makes dumb,
  Wondered if the dawn had come,—
The time to deck their plumes and sing.
In the grove the whip-poor-will
Forgot his story, and sat still:
But all who tell a tale of pain
Know well the place to begin again.

Music on a waveless stream
Where the stars and moonshine gleam,

While the light oar noiseless dips,
And then, lifting, brightly drips,
As if hung with pearl-strings rare,
Caught from the water-spirits' hair;
Then the music-freighted boat
Seems some fairy ark afloat,
Filled with groups of airy elves
Playing to delight themselves,
Blowing marvellous instruments,
With a thrill of joy intense,
Until the sounds that ring afar
Seem blown from many a clarion star;
Or as the thin rays of the moon,
   By some marvellous alchemy,
   Were changed from light to melody,
One-half lustre, one-half tune;
Or as the veil of the other world
Were partly lifted, partly furled,
   And underneath the soft notes born
   In the eternal fields of morn
Were wafted, on the wings of bliss,
Out of that realm into this.

Such were the sounds there heard to flow
From off· the winding stream below,—

Till suddenly a clattering steed
Dashed up the road in furious speed;
But soon the checking rein was drawn,
And now the rider gained the lawn.

And into Berkley's ear apart
He breathed a word that thrilled his heart;
And then from group to group it passed,
Quaking the breast from first to last:
Something about a rebel troop,
Like an eagle, soon to swoop;
How some of that obnoxious clan,
With horrid noise of horn and pan,[1]
Had borne in mockery up and down,
   In a rough and jolting car,
The noisiest Tory of the town,
   And only spared the plumes and tar
Because they deemed the honor due
To loyalists of deeper hue.
And it was said, and well believed,
And much the king's supporters grieved,
That many a secret rebel band
Was swiftly forming through the land;
Nor could the wisest well divine
The object of their full design,

But knew it much behooved them each
To be prepared or out of reach.
And—who could tell?—before they knew,
Some lawless and marauding crew—
None guessed their number or their power—
Might choose in such a festive hour
To burst into their midst and lay
A tax which it were hard to pay.

Scarce was the warning heard before
There was swift mounting at Berkley door,
And jostling hurry down roads of dust,
As if they fled from a thunder-gust!
They swept along the highway white,
    Like autumn leaves before the wind
    Which heralds the drowning storm behind,
And round the far hill passed from sight.

V.

THE UNWELCOME.

PROUD Berkley, while his arm was placed
Around his daughter's slender waist,
As up the lawn they swiftly paced,
Called loudly to his men in haste
To make the outer gates secure,
To bar and lock the stable-door,
Then loose the iron kennel-check
From off the savage mastiff's neck.

But scarce their feet had pressed the floor
Beside the open entrance-door,
When still he heard the revelling din
Of some who drank and laughed within.
Then cried the host, in gayer strain,
" It seems some lingering guests remain,

To praise those old Burgundian casks
Or compliment the Rhenish flasks.
This suits me well. I'll bid them stay
And revel till the break of day;
For where such manly mirth is made
No rebel band will dare invade."

He paced the hall like a generous host,
  And laughed to hear the loud uproar,
  Then cried, as he swung the festive door,
" Fill up, my friends, to a loyal toast !
  Fill high !"—but, at the sight revealed,
  Some sudden paces backward reeled,
  Like a stunned warrior on the field,
And stood a moment dumb and lost,
Like one who meets a midnight ghost.
Then stammered, "If my sight be true,
This is an honor scarcely due.
To what may I ascribe, strange sirs,
The presence of such visitors ?"

" To what," cried one, with the voice of a gale
  That laughs through an Alleghanian pine,
  " But to drink your health in good red wine
Till its hue returns to your cheek so pale ?"

And then the dozen sturdy men
Laughed, and brimmed their cups again,
And drained them to the hearty toast
Of Berkley Manor and its host. .

'Twas hard to see his dear old wines,
The heart's blood of the noblest vines,
Poured by a rough and sunburnt hand
To nourish the souls of a rebel band.
He heard the very wine's heart throb
As it flowed from the flask with a sigh and a sob;
The bubbles that wept around each rim
Looked with imploring eyes at him.

Then swelled that gusty voice once more,
As the speaker rose full six feet four:—
"That loyal toast you left unsaid,
To spare your breath, I propose instead;
And let the craven, who dares, resist
To drink the toast of a loyalist!"

Sir Hugh a moment felt relieved:
That word,—perchance he had been deceived;
They surely could no rebels be
Who proffered toasts to loyalty.

A goblet into his hand was thrust,
Brimming and dripping, and drink he must.

" Here's to our royal governors,
And every man who such prefers!
May Heaven on their advancement smile
In their speedy return to their native isle!"

Before his sense the words explained,
The lifted cup was wellnigh drained.
Then burst the intruders' laughter-roar,
    While stood the host with bewildered brain.
They rose and bowed, and said no more,
And now behind them slammed the door:
    He heard them descend the river-lane
With laugh and song, and all was o'er.
They had come like a sudden burst of rain,
And, like a gust, withdrew again,—
Their voices dying beyond the lawn,
Like rumbling clouds when the storm is gone.

Then in chagrin he dashed the glass
Down to the floor, a shattered mass,
And glared thereon, till, laughing, came,
Queen of the keys, the brave house-dame,—

A woman tall and somewhat sere,
But, like October, calm and clear;
Her dark eye still retained its ray,
Her hair its gloss, though touched with gray.
She cried, "You had strange guests to-night,
And such not often you invite:
Did but the world know who were here,
Yours would a rebel name appear."

To which Sir Hugh, with anger red,
"May a thousand plagues light on each head!
I cannot guess what men they be:
   I only know they drank my wine;—
   Would they might hang, a scarecrow line,
On the next lightning-blasted tree!"

Hulda replied, "Unless I err,
   I heard a voice I have heard before:
Each tone of his is a clinging burr,
That from the memory will not stir.—
   Though it is full ten years, or more,
   Since last I heard his laughter-roar,
   Or his great stride along the floor,
I would know, though twice as long it were,
Ringbolt, the wilful wagoner."

Then, in silence and in gloom,
The proud man passed to his private room,
And paced the floor, in spirit vexed,
With dusky fancies sore perplexed,—
Thought of his daughter, thought of his pride,
And of a hundred things beside.
But soon o'er his soul of turbulence
The quiet stole, and soothed the sense,
As silence with its hand at last
Smooths the pool where the storm has passed.

But hark!—was it the rising wind
Swinging the boughs on the window-blind?
Or chimney-swallows come anew,
    And talking in the sooty cavern,
Conversing as room-mate travellers do
    Ere they go to sleep in a wayside tavern?
Or was it some burglarious crew,
    With many a stealthy gouge and scratch,
Working their way from screw to screw,
    Mining around the bolt and latch,
With jar and screech, by sure degrees,
Or torturing locks with skeleton keys?

His heart beat loud: he spake no word,
But seized two pistols and a sword;

With cautious hand he oped the door,—
It creaked as it never creaked before,—
Then descended the stair; in his soul he vowed
He never knew them to crack so loud.

At every step he seemed to hear
The noises more distinct and near;
Now at the pistol-pans he tapped,
And cocked the flints,—how loud they snapped!—
Then followed the sounds with breathless care,
Here encountered a table, and there a chair,
Till it seemed as if to retard his pace
Each article had changed its place.

The wave of every curtain's fold
Now made his trembling heart less bold,
Lest, issuing from the midnight air,
His phantom bride should meet him there,
With wild mysterious eyes to peer
Into his shuddering soul of fear.

But now he gained the parlor-door
The noise was louder than before,—
A strange, mad music,—a grate,—a jar,—
Like a maniac trying to tune a guitar. ·

7*

By inch and by inch, he opened the door,
Saw long phantom windows stretch over the floor,
Made by the moon, and in the full flood,
Up at the end where the golden harp stood,
Beheld—and his heart strangely thrilled at the
    sight—
The cause of the noises, the source of his fright.

He gazed with anger mixed with joy,
As he beheld the marvellous boy,—
Anger at the fears unbounded,
Joy that they had proved unfounded:
One long relieving breath he drew,
Then gazed with silent, steadfast view.

Close to the harp the urchin prest
And clasped it fondly to his breast,
Then softly o'er his fingers stirred,
To wake the tones he late had heard;
Now stopped among the bass perplexed,
Then tried the tinkling treble next;
Now over all his wild hands sped,
And then, despairing, he shook his head;
His large eyes, wondering, seemed to say
The music had gone with the maid away.

Then he arose, with puzzled air,
And gazed upon the pictures there,
Marvelling much that such things were,
All so alive, and yet no stir:
And now he climbed into the niche
Where stood the suit of armor rich,
With golden tracery embossed,
And gazed on it in wonder lost,
From head to foot, with searching scan,
Surveyed the marvellous iron man;
Then, with a hand that nothing feared,
The visor carefully upreared,—
While Berkley saw, with a shudder of dread,
The horrid yawn of that iron head,—
Looked calmly in, and nothing saw,
Then closed it, having felt no awe.

Methinks to the angel of Peace 'twould be
A charmed and sacred sight to see
A child by an offcast coat of war,
Who dreamed not what 'twas fashioned foi.
Heaven send the time when bloody Mars
Shall only be known among the stars,
And his armor, with its thousand scars,
In a niche, as a curious thing, be bound,
And peered into, and nothing found!

Oh, would some sweet bird of the South[2]
Might build in every cannon's mouth,
Till the only sound from its rusty throat
Should be the wren's or the bluebird's note,
That doves might find a safe resort
In the embrasures of every fort!

Again to the harp the urchin passed,
    And sat him down, subdued and tame,
And seeming overweighed at last,
    He leaned against the golden frame;
His black hair drooped along the strings,
Like a fainting night-bird's wings;
A long sigh heaved his tired breast,
And slumber soothed him into rest.

There, like a spirit bright and good,
The guardian moon above him stood:
She kissed his cheeks, caressed his hair,
And filled with happy dreams the air,
Till the smile which o'er his features strayed
The pleasure at his heart betrayed.

Sir Hugh approached the sleeping child,
And stood with wondering thoughts beguiled.

How beautiful the picture there!—
 The gold harp propping the weary head,
The flashing cords, the shadowy hair,
 And over all the moonshine shed !

That slumbering face, it touched his heart,
And bade the puzzled memories start;
He had seen it in a dream before,—
A dream long gone to come no more.

To keep the weary sleeper warm,
 He spread a mantle where he lay,
And pressed it softly round his form,
 Then turned with noiseless feet away,
And left him there to dream at large,
The shadows' and the white moon's charge.

VI.

THE RISING.

OUT of the North the wild news came,
Far flashing on its wings of flame,
Swift as the boreal light which flies
At midnight through the startled skies.

And there was tumult in the air,
  The fife's shrill note, the drum's loud beat,
And through the wide land everywhere
  The answering tread of hurrying feet,
While the first oath of Freedom's gun
Came on the blast from Lexington.
And Concord, roused, no longer tame,
Forgot her old baptismal name,
Made bare her patriot arm of power,
And swelled the discord of the hour.

The strife was loud, the time was wild,
When from the sky Heaven's favorite child,
Sweet Liberty, in joy descended;
   A veil of lightning round her clung,
   Whereon the stars of morning hung,
   While o'er her head Jove's eagle swung,
With all his thunderbolts attended.

She came with Victory hand in hand,
   Whose flashing eyes and streaming hair
And gleaming robes and flaming brand
   Shot splendor through the dusky air,
And gladdened the awakening land.

Wild was the night; but wilder still
   The day which saw those sisters bright,
   In all their beauty and their might,
   Hanging above the battle-stroke,
   Waving like banners through the smoke
That veiled the heights of Bunker Hill.
The field was wellnigh won, when, lo!
From the enraged and reeling foe
Another charge, another blow,
   That reached and smote the patriot chief.
Pale Liberty recoiled a pace,
And for a moment veiled her face;

While Victory o'er her hero prest,
And wildly wept on Warren's breast
  The first tears of her grief.
Alas! that moment was her cost :—
When she looked up, the field was lost.

"Lost? lost?" she cried.   "It shall not be,
  While Justice holds her throne on high!
By Heaven! for every martyr dead,
For every sacred drop here shed
From out the brave hearts of the free,
  The foe shall doubly bleed and die!"

Such was the voice that fiercely rung
  From brave New England's rocks and pines;
Such were the notes that echo flung
Far southward, from its clarion tongue,
  Through all the Alleghanian lines;
And every homestead heard the call,
And one great answer flamed through all.

Each sacred hearthstone, deep and wide,
  Through many a night glowed bright and full;
The matron's great wheel at its side
  No more devoured the carded wool,

And now the maiden's smaller wheel
  No longer felt the throbbing tread,
But stood beside the idle reel
  Among its idle flax and thread.
No more the jovial song went round,
  No more the ringing laugh was heard;
But every voice had a solemn sound,
  And some stern purpose filled each word.

The yeoman and the yeoman's son,
  With knitted brows and sturdy dint,
Renewed the polish of each gun,
  Re-oiled the lock, reset the flint;
And oft the maid and matron there,
While kneeling in the firelight glare,
Long poured, with half-suspended breath,
The lead into the moulds of death.

The hands by Heaven made silken soft
  To soothe the brow of love or pain,
Alas! are dulled and soiled too oft
  By some unhallowed earthly stain;
But under the celestial bound
No nobler picture can be found
Than woman, brave in word and deed,
Thus serving in her nation's need:

8

Her love is with her country now,
Her hand is on its aching brow.

THE BRAVE AT HOME.

I.

The maid who binds her warrior's sash
    With smile that well her pain dissembles,
The while beneath her drooping lash
    One starry tear-drop hangs and trembles,
Though Heaven alone records the tear,
    And Fame shall never know her story,
Her heart has shed a drop as dear
    As e'er bedewed the field of glory !

II.

The wife who girds her husband's sword,
    Mid little ones who weep or wonder,
And bravely speaks the cheering word,
    What though her heart be rent asunder,
Doomed nightly in her dreams to hear
    The bolts of death around him rattle,
Hath shed as sacred blood as e'er
    Was poured upon the field of battle !

III.

The mother who conceals her grief
　　While to her breast her son she presses,
Then breathes a few brave words and brief,
　　Kissing the patriot brow she blesses,
With no one but her secret God
　　To know the pain that weighs upon her,
Sheds holy blood as e'er the sod
　　Received on Freedom's field of honor!

––––––––––

Within its shade of elm and oak
　　The church of Berkley Manor stood:
There Sunday found the rural folk,
　　And some esteemed of gentle blood.
In vain their feet with loitering tread
　　Passed mid the graves where rank is naught:
　　All could not read the lesson taught
In that republic of the dead.

How sweet the hour of Sabbath talk,
　　The vale with peace and sunshine full,
Where all the happy people walk,
　　Decked in their homespun flax and wool!

Where youths' gay hats with blossoms bloom;
  And every maid, with simple art,
  Wears on her breast, like her own heart,
A bud whose depths are all perfume;
While every garment's gentle stir
Is breathing rose and lavender.

There, veiled in all the sweets that are
  Blown from the violet's purple bosom,
The scent of lilacs from afar,
  Touched with the sweet shrub's spicy blossom,
Walked Esther; and the rustic ranks
Stood on each side like flowery banks,
To let her pass,—a blooming aisle,
Made brighter by her summer smile:
On her father's arm she seemed to be
The last green bough of that haughty tree.

The pastor came; his snowy locks
  Hallowed his brow of thought and care;
And, calmly as shepherds lead their flocks,
  He led into the house of prayer.
Forgive the student Edgar there
If his enchanted eyes would roam,
  And if his thoughts soared not beyond,

And if his heart glowed warmly fond
Beneath his hopes' terrestrial dome.
To him the maiden seemed to stand,
　　Veiled in the glory of the morn,
　　At the bar of the heavenly bourne,
A guide to the golden holy land.
When came the service' low response,
　　Hers seemed an angel's answering tongue;
　　When with the singing choir she sung,
　　O'er all the rest her sweet notes rung,
　　As if a silver bell were swung
Mid bells of iron and of bronze.

At times, perchance,—oh, happy chance!—
　　Their lifting eyes together met,
　　Like violet to violet,
Casting a dewy greeting glance.
For once be Love, young Love, forgiven,
　　That here, in a bewildered trance,
　　He brought the blossoms of romance
And waved them at the gates of heaven.

The pastor rose: the prayer was strong;
The psalm was warrior David's song;
The text, a few short words of might,—
" The Lord of hosts shall arm the right!"

He spoke of wrongs too long endured,
Of sacred rights to be secured;
Then from his patriot tongue of flame
The startling words for Freedom came.
The stirring sentences he spake
Compelled the heart to glow or quake,
And, rising on his theme's broad wing,
  And grasping in his nervous hand
  The imaginary battle-brand,
In face of death he dared to fling
Defiance to a tyrant king.

Even as he spoke, his frame, renewed
In eloquence of attitude,
Rose, as it seemed, a shoulder higher;
Then swept his kindling glance of fire
From startled pew to breathless choir;
When suddenly his mantle wide
His hands impatient flung aside,
And, lo! he met their wondering eyes
Complete in all a warrior's guise.[3]

A moment there was awful pause,—
  When Berkley cried, "Cease, traitor! cease!
  God's temple is the house of peace!"
The other shouted, "Nay, not so,

When God is with our righteous cause:
  His holiest places then are ours,
  His temples are our forts and towers
That frown upon the tyrant foe:
In this the dawn of Freedom's day
There is a time to fight and pray!"

And now before the open door—
  The warrior-priest had ordered so—
The enlisting trumpet's sudden soar
Rang through the chapel, o'er and o'er,
  Its long reverberating blow,
So loud and clear, it seemed the ear
Of dusty death must wake and hear.
And there the startling drum and fife
Fired the living with fiercer life;
While overhead, with wild increase,
Forgetting its ancient toll of peace,
  The great bell swung as ne'er before:
It seemed as it would never cease;
And every word its ardor flung
From off its jubilant iron tongue
  Was, "WAR! WAR! WAR!"

"Who dares"—this was the patriot's cry,
  As striding from the desk he came—

"Come out with me, in Freedom's name,
For her to live, for her to die?"
A hundred hands flung up reply,
A hundred voices answered, "*I!*"

VII.

THE WREATH.

How sweet it is when day is new,
And Summer is bathed in her young dew,
To contemplate, 'twixt sun and sod,
Each miracle that tells of God !

Thus Edgar mused in dreamy mood,
Next morn, on the upland solitude,
As, slowly pacing, he gained the site
Of the one great oak that crowned the height.
He threw him on a mossy mound,
   His whole soul flooded with the sense
   Of that delightful recompense
Which ever in the fields is found,
Which lifts the heart when tempest-bowed,
And sets the rainbow on the cloud.

He saw the river where it flowed
Under the morn, a golden road,—
Saw ships upon that highway free
Moving out to a boundless sea.
He saw the mist-dispelling sun
Mount, proudly conscious there was none
Sceptred beside himself, to hold
High state upon that throne of gold,
And thought of Freedom's glorious light
Conquering the dull mists of night.
He saw the moon with anxious stare
Walk down the cloudless western air,
Seeking the stars with pale dismay,
　　Like a shepherdess whose flocks
From the fields have gone astray
　　Among dusky woods and rocks,
In the wilderness to roam,
Till the eve shall bring them home.
But he thought decaying Tyranny
　　Might search for his lost flock in vain:
Those stars now seeking to be free
　　No gloomy eve should bring again.

Long, long he gazed on Berkley Hall,
And then on his native cottage small,—

The one embowered in tall, proud trees,
The one with its woodbine porch and bees;
And never before they struck his sense
With such a hopeless difference.
He felt how often heart from heart
Are kept by the mason's walls apart,
Even though the doors were open, free,
As Wealth can afford his doors to be.

Gliding along the garden-walks,
Gathering blossoms from the stalks,
He saw the heiress of Berkley Hall,
And fancied he heard the rise and fall
Of the melody he knew must be
Flooding her lips incessantly:
For song was native to her tongue
As to a runnel valeward flung,
As wind to a cloud, as mist to a fall,
As dew to the rose, and as sunshine to all.
His full heart ached with love's sweet pain,
Like a sealed fountain, charged with rain,
That longs to sing in the summer air,
Yet faints in its cavern of despair.

From plot to bower, from vase to vase,
Down to the very garden-base,

He watched her gliding, fawnlike pace;
The branches bowed to her forehead fair
And shed their blooms on her golden hair.

Oh, what is so like an embodied May
As a frolic maiden, with laughter gay,
Chasing her fancies as they flit
Out of her heart of innocent wit,
Shrining herself in the blowing bowers,
Her tresses flecked with falling flowers?
O Heaven, when I am old and bent,
And into the valley deathward sent,
Be the last sweet vision which charms my way
A breathing, bright, embodied May,
That, while I lean upon my staff,
I may see her smile and hear her laugh,
That my heart may be fresh, till its life is null,
With the sun and the dew of the beautiful!

A tree blown bright with summer blooms,
    O'errun with honeysuckle-vines,
A very fount of sweet perfumes,
Stood in the garden, where the bees
    Toiled ever in these murmurous mines:
And Edgar might have envied these;

For some which mined that odorous store
Brought back their sweets to his father's door.

Around this tree a stairway led
Into the branches overhead,
And there, mid spreading antler-boughs,
 A little room was fitted well,
Where a votaress might make her vows
 Secure within her flowery cell.

Such a one there stands to-day
In a poet's garden far away,
Where on many an afternoon,
His great soul full of marvellous tune
Cloistered among flowers and leaves,
He sings, and all the world receives.

Lightly up the vine-like stair,
 Light of heart and light of foot,
Flitted the maiden into the bower.
Never in enchanted air
Held a vine so fair a flower
 Or tree so sweet a fruit.

She sat; the flickering sun and shade
Like wingéd sprites about her played;

The wren peered in with curious eye,
The bluebird carolled closely by,
The robin from her nest above
Looked, and resumed her task of love.

The maiden's lap was full of flowers,
Culled from the lavish garden-bowers.
Mid these her fingers gayly played,
Entwining happy shade with shade,
And, as she wrought the flowers among,
Her sweet thoughts rippled into song.

I.

The blue-eyed lady of the morn,
　　While she wreathes her flowers of light,
　　Knows for whom those flowers are bright,
By whom they shall be worn :
She knows the golden locks of Day
Shall bear that flashing wreath away.

II.

Though she knows their shape and hue
　　May be crushed and tarnished soon,
　　And the battle-heat of noon
Waste their precious dew,

Yet she knows when day is through
He shall wear his wreath anew.

III.

Would I knew some hero now!
 He should wear the wreath I make.
 Not for mine, but Freedom's sake,
I would deck his brow;
Should his arm victorious prove,
He should wear the wreath of love.

IV.

Should he fall, I would outgrieve
 All who ever grief possessed;
 I would weep upon his breast,
Overveiled like dewy Eve,
And above my hero dead
Pour my tears till life had fled.

The music on its golden wing
Dropt from those dewy lips of spring;
Scarce had the cadence ceased to flow,
 There was a sound of footsteps fleet,
And suddenly, with cheeks aglow,
 Young Edgar knelt before her feet.

She started with surprise—not fear—
To find the stranger youth so near.
He read the question in her eye,
And, ere she spoke, he made reply :—

" Oh, lady, if I err, forgive :
I know not, scarcely, if I live,
Or that it is my soul is drawn
By witching music, on and on,
To kneel to thee in holier guise,
While its poor dwelling yonder lies !
I was as one within a land
   Where all he sees is dead and sere,
Who droops with thirst, till near at hand
   He hears a fountain singing clear,
Then, without further question, flies
To find the spring which life supplies.
In sooth, the music drew me near,
And left me, lady, kneeling here.
I heard the wish your song expressed,
And echo answered in my breast,
Oh, bid me wear that wreath you make,
For thine as well as Freedom's sake !"

The maiden's lips no word replied ;
   But still the youth could well descry

That there was pleasure in her eye
And that her cheek was double-dyed.

A moment, with extended hands,
    She held the precious wreath in air,
Looked in his face her sweet commands,
    Then pressed it on her hero's hair,
And would have fled with girlish bound,
But suddenly a whirring sound
Made her light foot recoil a pace,
And drove the roses from her face.

A wingéd arrow fiercely near
Had lightly grazed the stranger's ear,
Dislodged one garland-bloom, and sunk
Quivering in the gnarled trunk,
And firmly there the angry dart
Transfixed the blossom's odorous heart.

Her flashing eye the maiden turned:
One hurried glance the truth discerned.
Near by, upon the gravel path,
Holding his attitude of wrath,
The wild-eyed boy defiant stood.
His black hair in a flashing flood

Flung back, the quivering bow's advance,
  The right hand to the shoulder drawn,
The knitted brow, the fiery glance
  Still following where the dart had gone,—
He looked the great Apollo's child,
Born in a forest dark and wild.

A moment thus his posture kept
  The young soul burning in his face,
  Then suddenly, as in disgrace,
He flung him on the grass and wept.

Her heart was moved, her pity stirred :
She fled to him as flies a bird
Which hears its lonely fledgling call ;
  She raised his head, smoothed back his hair,
  Looked in his eyes of wild despair.
He smiled, and she forgave him all,
Then led him calmly up the lawn,
Glanced at the bower,—the youth was gone.

Young Edgar passed the garden-gate
With dazzled brain and heart elate ;
The very landscape seemed to quiver,
  As if the burning pulse of love

Was throbbing in the sky above,
Thrilling the forest, field, and river.

His spirit's wings had sudden birth;
He felt beneath no heavy earth:
He trod as on a field of air,
And the flowers like stars shone everywhere.

Down through the grove he gained the stream,
Which flowed before him like a dream,
Its ripples whispering to the shore,
And love their burden evermore;
Stream, flower, and tree, and breeze, and bird,
Were eloquent with that one word.

He knelt, with very joy o'erweighed,
Beneath a flowering poplar's shade,
And seized the coronal and kissed
    The blossoms,—(Love must have his will,)—
    And held them to his lips until
His eyes were full of blissful mist,
Through which the bright scene brighter shone
In iris colors all his own.
Then solemnly the flowers he prest
Beneath the crossed hands on his breast,

And cried, "In face of Death and Heaven,
This sacred wreath by thee was given,
 And it shall not dishonored be!
Here, in face of Heaven and Death,
I pledge my life, my latest breath,
 To Freedom and to thee!"

" A valiant oath,—and nobly sworn!"
 Exclaimed a voice of thunder near;
"And, if it be no idle boast,
Go forth to-day, and take your post:
For hark! 'tis Freedom's bugle-horn
 Which summons you from here!

Mount yonder steed,—unless I err,
He will not wait for whip or spur,—
And I have one as good beside.
'Tis well: we both have far to ride."

The youth sprang up.   The speaker's height
Loomed o'er him like a cloud of night:
The palm on Edgar's shoulder flung
In friendship, wellnigh made him reel:
The pledging right hand ached and stung,
 Grasped in the wagoner's grip of steel.

"Our place of secret rendezvous,"
He said, "is only known to few,—
A cavern in a wild ravine,
  Hid by the friendly oak and vine,
  Where naught is heard but the Brandywine,
Which rolls a shadowy flood between;
A hidden place, that well might be
  The stronghold of a robber crew:
Of such persuasion are not we,
  Save in our royal tyrant's view.

Your guide I cannot be to-day;
My course lies far another way;
But there is one will guide you true:
  Already, with a heart of joy,
By yonder wall he waits for you,
  Henceforth your friend,—the frolic boy.
Mount you, and place the youth behind,—
  The wildest steed may carry double,—
And in the holsters you will find
  Two trusty guards in case of trouble.

And when you meet the wild-eyed dame
  Who reigns within our secret place,
  If she looks strangely in your face,
Speak kindly,—simply name my name,—

That my command has brought you hence,
　No further it behooves to know :
'Twere well you give her no offence :
　She may be—— Well, no matter : go."

They parted, and the youth obeyed,
And when the friendly evening laid
Concealment over rock and wave,
He gained the river and the cave.[4]

PART II.

I.

THE YOUNG PATRIOT.

THREE years the flying sun and shade
  O'er Berkley Hall their change had cast,
Since the wild urchin and the maid
  Within its loyal portal passed.
Two years the invader's war-alarms
  Had waked the land, which still defied,
And oft the gleam of patriot arms
  From Berkley's turret was descried.

Upon his central roof a tower
  Rose and o'erlooked the country wide,—
A place scarce fit for lady's bower;
  For there was seen, on every side,
Many a cast-off coat of war,
Helmet and sword, with hack and scar,

With guns and pistols crosswise hung,
O'er which the dust of years was flung.

And there through many a changeful hour
    The anxious father and the maid
    Through telescopic glass surveyed
The impending cloud of battle lower;
They watched it move o'er land and stream,
    They saw the white sails come and go,
And all the flashing splendor gleam
    Along the bristling plains below.

There had they gazed through one long day,
Watching an army glide away
Beyond the city's western side,—
So far, the line was scarce descried;
But Esther knew a nation's trust
Marched there in that long cloud of dust.

"Thank Heaven!" the loyalist exclaimed,
"They are gone!—our city is reclaimed,
And England's banner now may fly,
To gladden every loyal eye!"

But now a voice, like a clarion clear,
Rang laughing in the speaker's ear :—

"I saw him! and your vaunt is vain;
I saw him and his warrior train:
Had you beheld that hero host,
Your fears had not allowed the boast."

Who dared in Berkley's presence proud
Speak rebel words so fierce and loud?
   Sir Hugh his hand in anger laid
   Upon the handle of his blade;
But when he saw the wild-eyed boy,
And gazed upon his face of joy,
   The vengeance in his breast was stayed.

Then, with a tremor on his tongue,
   While something paler grew his cheek,
As some retarding memory clung
   On the rebuke he fain would speak,
He said, "Rash boy, beware! beware!
   You put my kindness to the proof.
Is it for this my three years' care
   Has sheltered you beneath my roof?
Is it for this——" He said no more:
   He saw the tear, the brow of pain,—
A look which he had seen before,
   And one he would not see again.

"Nay, Ugo, nay!" the maiden cried,
    Her two hands clasping his between;
Her tender eyes to his replied,
    And straightway all his troubled mien
Grew bright, as when the iris form
Glows on the cloud that threatened storm.
"Nay, Ugo, nay: speak out, and say
The things which you have seen to-day."

"Him have I seen," the boy exclaimed,
"Yes, him!—what needs he to be named?
The world has only one broad sun,
And Freedom's world but Washington."

Even while he spake that fiery word,
    The stripling's stature seemed to grow;
All his young hero spirit stirred
Sent to his cheek the warrior glow:
Save the same look, which knew no awe,
    Learned on his native mountains wild,
    You scarcely longer saw the child
Which thrice a twelvemonth past you saw.

"Him have I seen!—oh, sight to cheer
    The patriot when he bleeding lies,

To kindle hope and scatter fear,
  And light new fire in dying eyes!

His way with banners waved and burned,
  The welkin rang with patriot cheers,
From every window fondly yearned
  Bright eyes that spoke their joy in tears.

And music round his pathway flung
  Its gladness in a silver shower,
And over all the great bells swung,
  Shouting their joy from every tower.

The snow-white war-horse he bestrode
  Stept conscious, with a soul of flame,
As if he knew his master rode
  Straight to the glorious gates of Fame.

The coldest gazer's heart grew warm,
  And felt no more its indecision;
For every soul which saw that form
  Grew larger to contain the vision.

I watched the long, long ranks go by,[5]
And saw defiance in every eye;

10*

And every soldier true and staunch
Wore in his cap a vernal branch,
As Victory had placed it there
For Fame to twine about his hair.

Oh, how the wild heart sent its blood
Through all the frame, a throbbing flood,
To see those spirits, true and tried,
Who crossed at night the roaring tide,
What time the grinding gulfs of ice
Made all the desperate peril thrice,
When nothing but a patriot's fire
Could breast the winter's bitter ire,—
Who barefoot trod December's snow,
And took the hirelings at a blow !

You should have seen that stream of life
　Westward go and eastward come,
Thrilled and cheered by the startling fife,
　Throbbed through and through by many a drum.

There, on his charger fierce and tall,
　A fiery stallion black as night,
His bold front overtopping all,—
　A very tower along the right,—

With eye that death could not deter,
  His rifle o'er his shoulder flung,
  Two pistols in his holsters hung,
Rode Ringbolt, the wild wagoner.

They who have seen that mighty hand
  And heard the swearing of his whip
  May well conceive the giant grip
That wielded the commanding brand.

There, like a son by his warrior sire,
  And mounted on a steed as good,
His eye aflame with patriot fire,
  His cheek aflush with patriot blood,
Rode Edgar, and the leaves of green
Set in his cap had a rose between;
I knew not what the intent might be:
Perchance 'twas there for memory.

And after these a hundred more,
  Obedient to the wagoner's word,
As fierce a band as ever bore
  Through fire and flood the avenging sword.
These were his 'mountain eagles,'—these,
  So often seen a flying cloud

That sweeps the hills through forest-trees,
　Following their leader loud,—
　　A cloud whose form
　　Is a whirlwind storm,
　　When on the flanks
　　Of the foeman's ranks
It breaks from upland covert near,
　And pours its sudden bolts of wrath,
　Then gains anew the secret path
Ere it is said, 'The storm is here!'
Pale wonder strikes the columns wide,
　And, ere the foe can count his slain,
Thundering down the other side
　The swooping tempest strikes again.

But yesterday I heard their tramp,
　And saw their chargers dashing down,
　Each wild mane like a banner blown:
　They swam the river, leapt the creek,
And o'er the near hills gained the camp,
　Bearing the news from Chesapeake."

So spake the youth.　The maid near by
Sat gazing in his clear, dark eye,
As if she saw in its depths, anew,
The whole bright pageant passing through.

But Berkley frowned his blackest frown,
As that would put the rebel down,
And cried, "Well, sir, and is this all?
    The picture you would have us view
    Is rare, and colored somewhat new :
Methinks 'twere easier to recall
    That barefoot, tattered, hungry crew
Quartered but now near Berkley Hall.
The farmers' planted fields forlorn
Will make a poor return of corn,
    And thievish birds wax fat, I fear,
    Since all the scarecrows volunteer !"
And he laughed the bitter laugh of scorn,
    So grating to a patriot's ear.

"You know so well how a rebel feels
    Fresh from his sty of mire and straw,
While dangling, tangling 'twixt his heels
    Is dragged the sword he dares not draw :
Gird on this brand, and let us see
The brave young rebel you would be !"
So speaking, he took from its place of dust
A blade whose scabbard was thick with rust :--
"And this chapeau, for many a year
Untouched among the cobwebs here,—

The webs may serve you yet for lint;
  This ancient gun,
    With rust o'errun,—
It matters not the loss of flint;
A pistol or so to grace your side;
This old flask, too :—be naught denied
To deck you in your warrior pride!
Behold you now!   By Heaven, you stand
As fair a rebel as walks the land!"

Again the bitter laugh was flung
From off the old man's scornful tongue.

The youth a moment glared in doubt,
  Reddening like one who stands at bay;
But presently burst his laughter-shout,
  And, crying, "Then be it as you say!"
Wildly sprang from the tower away.

They heard him descend the echoing stair,
And Berkley stood with wondering air,
Listening with wide eyes and lips,
  Like a traveller on Vesuvius' top
  When his adventurous hand lets drop
A stone into the yawning pit,

From rock to rock he hears it flit,
Till the noises die in a far eclipse.

But, when the clattering sounds were past,
Sir Hugh stood with the look aghast
Of a sire who has held his favorite boy,
In frolic, only to fright and annoy,
Over a precipice wild and deep,
When, with a sudden and desperate leap,
The child is gone! and the father stands,
Stunned and staring, with empty hands.

.

II.

RUST ON THE SWORD.

O HAPPY and secure retreat,
  Dear Valley, home of many friends!
I envy even the hurried feet
  Which fancy through your quiet sends!

There led of old the Cambrian swain
  His flock by flowery brook and rill,
Flinging across the summer plain
  The song he learned on Snowdon's hill,—
Perchance some fragmentary strain
  Of ancient Merlin's wizard skill.

His language now no longer breathes
  Its strange, wild music through the scene,
But here and there a name still wreathes
  His memory in perpetual green.

Tredyffrin, Caln, and Nantmeal, hold
Traditions of those sires of old;
While Uwchlan, in her inmost vale,
May hear at eve some Cambrian tale.

Though many a brave ancestral name
    Has, starlike, in the distance set,
Still thou hast others dear to Fame,
    Forgetful Time shall not forget,—
Bright memories which shall long remain
    Cherished by every patriot breast,—
    That of the calm-browed painter West,
And his, the fiery-hearted Wayne;
And in thy scientific bowers
    Are those which fear nor frost nor sun:
There, written with immortal flowers,
    Are found such names as Darlington.
Nor dost thou need my hand to fling
    The poet's offering on thy shrine:—
Among thy vales sweet minstrels sing
    Like thine own flashing Brandywine.
From Kennet, Taylor's soaring strain
    Rings like a silver bugle round,
As if on that near battle-plain
    Some herald's clarion he had found.

11

'Twas midnight in the secret cave,
Darkness and silence reigning, save
The dreary muttering of the brands
    That flickered where a cauldron hung;
While dreaming near, with folded hands,
    A woman sat, no longer young :—
No longer young,—or rather say
Her first youth only passed away.
Her hair, as by a wind thrown back,
Was glossy still, and thick and black;
Her brow was clear, save where the brain
Had set its outward seal of pain.
Her cheek was tanned, her eye was bright
With something of unearthly light;
A string of mingled bead and shell,
Which seemed of woodland life to tell,
Entwined her head, and round her waist
A costly wampum belt was placed;
While on her tawny neck and arm
Hung amulet and bracelet charm.
Her robes of mingled cloth and fur
With beads and quills embroidered were:
And thus in her wild forest dress
She looked an Indian prophetess,
With still a something in her face,
    And something in her slender mien,

Beyond the finest savage grace
  That ever marked a chieftain's queen.

There sat she gazing, dreamy-eyed,
As if within the flame she spied
Visions of scenes long past and gone,
Or some strange pleasure yet to dawn.
But now her quick ear caught a sound,—
  A stealthy footfall drawing near:
A light hare tripping o'er the ground
  Would wake her eye, but not her fear:
  Still through the leaves it came more clear,—
Her hand was on the rifle laid,
Her quick glance pierced the cavern's shade;
But soon the well-known whisper came,
Giving the watchword and her name:—
"Hist, Nora!—hist! 'tis I!"—she bade
Young Ugo enter undismayed.

A moment in his laughing eye
  She gazed, then scanned his strange attire:
  His figure brightened by the fire,
His shadow looming darkly high,
The sword, the gun, the pistols, hat,—
With questioning look she stared thereat.

"Say, Ugo, say, where was the theft?
What loyalist have you bereft?"

. " No theft," the boy indignant cried,
   " But gift of one who bade me don
   These rebel arms, and urged me on,
Until, to please him, I complied;
But who, or where, or when, or how,
The question matters little now.
Come, Nora,—you were ever good,—
I only ask a little food,
. And then your helping hand to-night
To make this old sword somewhat bright;
While on these pistols I renew
The polish which is still their due,
And from the gun remove the crust
Of honorable dust and rust;
For well I know the time is near—
The scene, too, not o'er far from here—
When every weapon we can wield
Shall be most dear to Freedom's field."

She gave him food with generous hand,
And then essayed to cleanse the brand;
And, while she wrought the blade along,
She cheered her toiling hand with song.

SONG.

I.

Oh, sweet is the sound of the shuttle and loom
When the lilies of peace fill the land with perfume!
Then cheerily echoes the axe from the hill,
While the bright waters sing on the wheel of the mill,
And the anvil rings out like a bell through the day,
And the wagoner's song cheers his team on the way,
Till the bugles sound here, and the drums rattle there,
And the banners of War stream afar on the air.

II.

Then wild is the hour, and fearful the day,
When the shuttle is dropt for the sword and the fray,
When the woodman is felling a foe at each stroke,
And the miller is blackened with powder and smoke,
When the smith wields the blade in his terrible grip,
And the wagoner's rifle cracks true as his whip:
The bugles sound here, and the drums rattle there,
While the banners of War stream afar on the air.

III.

Our brave-hearted yeomen,—our lords of the soil,—
They reap where they sow the reward of their toil;

11*

In the broad field of labor their harvest is blithe,
Their favorite arms the plough, sickle, and scythe:
The plough and the sickle, the scythe and the flail,—
These, these are their weapons, with these they prevail,
Till the bugles sound here, and the drums rattle there,
And the banners of War stream afar on the air.

IV.

Then the plough-horse is mounted, and flies o'er the
    plain,
The blade is flung by in the grass or the grain,
And the hand that grew strong on the flail or the
    plough,   •
And battled alone with the harvest till now,
The rifle and sword can as steadily wield,
Till the harvest of foemen is swept from the field;
While the bugles sound here, and the drums rattle there,
And the banners of War stream afar on the air.

V.

Be God on our side in the season of dread!
Be His strength with the living, His peace with the
    dead;
His love shield the widow and orphan, His care
Soothe the parents whose sorrow shall whiten their
    hair;

Be success with the right when the struggle is through,
And the sword be returned to the ploughshare anew,
And no bugle sound here, and no drum rattle there,
While the banners of Peace stream afar on the air!

Thus, singing strenuously, she toiled
To cleanse the blade which Time had soiled.
The dull stains clung unto the steel,
    As they were spots of murderous red
Whose stubborn hue must needs reveal
    The crime when first that blood was shed.

She knelt before the midnight flame,
    Which seemed to leap with pleasure new:
She gazed,—a chill ran through her frame
    As if a spectre met her view:
She saw the Berkley arms and name
Slow struggling through the veil of rust,
Then swooned, and sank into the dust.

But Ugo's aid was instant there:
    He raised her head upon his knee,
Called her by name, smoothed back her hair,
Looked with a face of mute despair
    On hers of pallid agony.

At length a breath came full and deep,
And then, as one who walks in sleep
And sees with large unwavering eyes
Through veils of awful mysteries,
She stared, and sighed, "O Heaven! 'tis done!—
Where fought the two there stands but one:"
Then passed her hand across her brow,
   And looked in the o'erbending face,
Which still its pitying posture kept:—
"O Ugo, do not leave me now!"
   She groaned. "It is a dreary place!"
Then bowed her head and wept.

"Go, lay her on her couch apart!"
The deep voice made the hearers start.
She choked the tears back to her heart,
And mounted like a wounded deer
That hears its calling comrade near.

"Good Nora, we have much to do,"
Said Ringbolt, "yet no need of you.
Our eagle troop will soon be here:
They tether now their horses near.
The boy our sentinel watch can keep,
So to your couch a while and sleep.

Unless the storm should pass, or pause,
  Which hangs in thunder o'er the land,
  Ere set of many suns, your hand
May do good service in our cause.

All night the well-piled fire must glow,
  All night the molten lead be poured,
  Our guns re-cleaned, re-sharped the sword,
In honor of the approaching foe;
And if it be, as beldames say,
  The devil feasts when tyrants fall,
Let his infernal board straightway
  Be spread, with room enough for all!"

III.

A BURIAL.

ROUND all the wide horizon's bar
There lay no growing cloud to mar
   The brightness of the autumn day;
And yet the soft air felt the jar
Of thunder rolling from afar,[6]
   And shuddered in its pale dismay.

Berkley, with anxious eye and ear,
Stood on the southern porch to hear,
Disturbed with many a doubt and fear,
   As rolled the distant roaring in;
Then to his tower he mounted high,
And searched through all the cloudless sky:
All, all was clear, while still came by
   The rumble of the constant din.

Was direful war the sudden source?
Was it for this the rebel force
Had ta'en but now their southward course?
  The sound his fears too well define!
It is, it is the cannon's mouth!
Its awful answer from the south
Bears tidings of the roaring ranks
That crash upon the trembling banks,
  The crimson banks, of Brandywine.

Pale Esther, in that gloomy tower,
Strained her sad vision's fruitless power:
On every sound she seemed to hear
  The shout and groan together swell;
At every burst that came more clear,
  She deemed her hero Edgar fell,—
Fell, and perchance had breathed his last
Long ere the death-announcing blast,
Speeding through miles of frighted air,
His dying sigh to her could bear.

Still hearkening, gazing far abroad,
  Some sign of triumph to discover,
All day she poured her prayer to God
  To shield her country and her lover.

And Berkley, listening to the fight,
Remembered Trenton's direful night,
And that it was the same fierce train
  Whose lengthy line he saw of late
Pour from the city o'er the plain,
  Led by a leader bold and great,
Who now upon that roaring field
Might cause once more their flag to yield.

His heart, misgiving, sank away,
Shuddering through the doubtful day:
· And should the rebels win, what then?—
The troops were bold and desperate men:
And he remembered with affright
The terrors of that startling night
What time a rude and lawless crew
  (All such he deemed the patriot lines)
Intruded on his midnight view
  And drank his dearest, noblest wines:
His frame was agued through and through
Lest that wild scene should come anew.

"Ho! gardener, hostler, coachman!—ho!
  Each man whose hand can wield a spade!
  A place of safety must be made:
Bring shovels, hoes, and picks, and show

How you can ply the digging trade."
When Berkley's will was thus conveyed,
Down came the gardener and his man,
The hostler and the hostler's lad,
The coachman and the footman ran,
And each his delving orders had.

"Dig me a pit!" the master cried,
"And let it be both deep and wide,
As 'twere a grave that might contain
A score or more of rebels slain.
But they for whom this grave is made
Belong unto a nobler grade,
With better blood than ever ran
In purple veins of outlaw clan.
Their royal genealogic lines
Come down the Old World's antique vines:
Ho, butler! my good sacristan,
Bear out our monarch king of wines,
Old Port, in all his purple pride,
With queenly Sherry at his side,
Followed by all their loyal train,
The brave, light-hearted German knights
Whose birth was on the Rhenish heights,
The well-beloved of Charlemagne,

12

And all those maids whose bright eyes glance
In memory of their native France.
Here, give them to their parent mould
    Till peace has stilled this rebel strife;
Then doubly bright and doubly bold
    Shall be their renovated life."

Sir Hugh, thus making mournful mirth,
    That poorly cloaked his trembling fear,—
    It may be with a secret tear,—
Consigned his precious wines to earth:
'Twas midnight ere they smoothed away
All traces where his treasures lay.

'Twas midnight, and a moon in heaven,
    And silence over stream and hill,
Save where the lone bird's song was given,
    Or aspens, with a whispering thrill,
Seemed sheltering some young wind benighted,
Late from the battle-field affrighted.
The moon which through the window gazed
    Saw Esther 'gainst her harp reclining,
Her pale and prayerful face upraised,
    And each eye with a tear-drop shining.

Her prophet-heart foreboding well
The fate which to that field befell,
Her fingers trembled on the string,
And thus her prayerful song took wing.

SONG.

I.

O God, o'er all this blooming earth
　　Is it with thine approving eye
That every flower of noble birth
　　Must bow to poisonous weeds, or die?

II.

Through all our pastures must there run
　　The bramble which no fruitage bears?
Must every field which loves the sun
　　Be arrogant with choking tares?

III.

Must every tree whose leaves divine
　　Were made in Freedom's air to spread
Be clasped by the obnoxious vine
　　Until its boughs are sapped and dead?

IV.

Wilt thou not send some mighty hand
    To sweep through these entangled walks,
To root the proud weeds from the land
    And burn the rank and thorny stalks?

A moment now she paused, and sighed,
    Her hand still on the quivering cords,
    As waiting the ensuing words,
When, at the open casement wide,
A voice in patriot tones replied :—

" Yes, God hath sent that arm of wrath :
    It sweeps the land with sword of fire ;
The poisonous weeds but strew his path
    To build Oppression's funeral pyre !"

Sweet is the sound when pardon calls
The prisoner from his dreary walls ;
And sweet the succoring voice must be
Which hails a sinking ship at sea ;
And dear the water's light when first
It greets the desert-pilgrim's thirst,

Or from the friendly helmet drips
To cool a fainting patriot's lips:
But not more sweet or dear than when
A fond heart hears and meets again
The voice and the responding eye
Of one, the dearest 'neath the sky,
Whom picturing fancy saw but now
With drooping head and bleeding brow,
Or heard the last-drawn sigh of pain
Which laid him with his comrades slain:
Her arm was round her hero prest,
Her head was on his happy breast.

IV.

THE FIGHT AT THE FORD.

WHEN passed the first wild burst of joy,—
That bliss which harbors no alloy,—
The maiden brushed aside the tear,
   And sighed, " Oh, Edgar, is it true?
And are you living, breathing here,
   Or is't a phantom cheats my view,
And leads me up this happy brink
To plunge me deeper when I sink?
Art sure that from the dreadful fray
You brought no bleeding wound away ?
Thank Heaven that fainting prayer can win
Its way above the battle-din !
But tell me what great deeds were done,
   How the red waves were backward tossed

Until the glorious field was won———"
 "Alas!" he answered, "it was lost!
And we retreat,—so deems the foe;
But soon his bleeding ranks shall know
 'Tis but the arrow drawing back
Upon the stubborn-bending bow,
To deal a fiercer, deadlier blow
 When vengeance speeds it on its track.

But how shall I describe the fray?
How word the horrors of the day
To suit a timid maiden's ear?
In sooth, the scenes are yet too near:
The roaring cannon and the strife,
With all those whirling ranks of life,
Sweep through my brain, a puzzled maze,
Confused within a cloudy haze:
It seems a wild and broken dream,
With transitory glimpse and gleam
 Of grappling groups, of bayonets' quiver,
Of flashing guns and sabre-stroke,
Caught through the openings of the smoke
 Upon some visionary river.

Wrapt in a friendly cloud of mist,
 At morn the wagoner led us out,

And, following our bold leader's shout,
We put the pickets oft to rout,
Oft trampling down a scouting list,
And oft upon the foeman's flanks
We dealt the blow their startled ranks
Scarce knew where to resist.

For hours we sailed from rear to front,
And down their side, from front to rear:
Death and confusion paid the brunt
Wherever we came near.
Anon was heard the opening roar
Which called us to the bristling shore;
And now the fearful scene was won
Where deadly gun replied to gun,
And pistol answered pistol flash,
And then the fiery, sudden dash
Of hand to hand, and sword to sword,
While in the stream, with plunge and splash,
Though thrice our number on us poured,
We dealt the thick foe crash for crash,
. And strove to hold the ford.

Now was the time you should have seen
Bold Ringbolt with his towering mien;

Have heard his voice, have seen his blow
  Which drove the heavy weapon home,
Each stroke of which unhorsed a foe,
And sent him reeling red below,
  Mid trampled waters crushed to foam.
But, oh, it would have touched your pride
Could you have seen at Ringbolt's side
  Our standard-bearer, young and bold,
  Fighting and grasping in his hold
  The banner whose unsullied fold
The foeman's rage defied!

But, sad to see, and sad to tell,
Brave Ugo's horse beneath him fell,
  The banner-boy went down.
A moment,—shall the horses' tread
Deal death upon his struggling head?
  A moment,—shall he drown?
No!—Ringbolt from his saddle leaps,
  His mighty arm is round him cast,
But still his fighting posture keeps,
  His blows fly strong and fast.

The rider who survives must grieve
That ere his brave steed strove to cleave

With rearing hoof that skull apart,
He fell an instant carcass slain,
Hewed wellnigh through from throat to mane,
    Or gashed unto the heart.

No arm with that great arm could cope,
    Whether or foot or fiery horse;
    But now, as with a tiger's force
    When battling to protect its young,
    Upon his steed again he sprung,
    While in his hold the boy still hung,
    And grasping, as with grip of death,
    The reins between his angry teeth,
To give his right arm clearing scope,
    There still his blade of battle swung,
    And on the pressing foemen flung
    The blow that to the invaders rung
The knell of many a hero's hope.

At last the overwhelming tide
    Of foemen pressed us slowly back;
    We did not turn, we did not slack
    Our heavy blows, or ever flinch,
    But, slowly backing, inch by inch,
We gained the other side.

But now was heard the roaring din
Of Wayne's artillery pouring in;
And while its iron torrent flowed,
  Leaving the foe enough to do,
  Along the highway we withdrew,
To breathe a little, and reload.

When Ugo wakened from his swoon,
Gathering his scattered senses soon,
  He sought the banner of his pride;
He looked through all the busy band,
And stared upon his empty hand,
  Then cast his eagle glances wide.
'Oh, death! oh, infamy!' he cried:
He saw it on the other side,
Beneath the invader's standard tied,
Heavily hanging, wet and tame,
Weeping as 'twere in grief and shame.

The hour was loud, but louder still
  Anon the rage of battle roared
Its wild and murderous will;
  · From Jefferis down to Wistar's ford,
  From Jones to Chads the cannon poured,
While thundered Osborne Hill.

Oh, ne'er before fled holy calm
   From out its sainted house of prayer
   So frighted through the trembling air
As from that shrine of Birmingham!

Oft through the opening cloud we scanned
The shouting leaders, sword in hand,
   Directing the tumultuous scene;
There galloped Maxwell, gallant Bland
   The poet-warrior, while between,
Ringing o'er all his loud command,
   Dashed the intrepid Greene.

Here Sullivan in fury trooped,
There Weedon like an eagle swooped,
With Muhlenberg,—where they were grouped
   The invader dearly earned his gains,—
And (where the mad should only be
The fiercest champion of the free)
   The loudest trumpet-call was Wayne's;
While in a gale of battle-glee,
   With rapid sword and pistol dealing
   The blows which set the foemen reeling,
Sped 'light-horse Harry Lee.'
And once or twice our eye descried,
Mid clouds a moment blown aside,

With lifted hand that well might wield
  The thunders of the storming field,
The JOVE of battle ride!
And every eye new courage won
Which gazed that hour on Washington.

'Twas now that, marvelling, we beheld
  Upon the rising summit near,
By every danger unrepelled,
  Confused by smoke and dust,—not fear,—
A form with wild and floating dress,
Which looked a battle-prophetess.
But when the veiling cloud went by,
We knew the face and flashing eye
Of Nora, and we heard her cry
  Of warning in that hour of need :—

'Speed, Ringbolt, to your leader speed!
And bid him know the stealthy foe
  With double strength comes up behind:
  It was but now I saw him wind
From out the valley road below.'

She ceased: a short and sudden scream
Escaped her breast, across the stream,

13

Far piercing through the veil of haze
Her fierce eyes sent their staring gaze,
And, following that stare, we saw,
With soul of wonder and of awe,
Where Porter and bold Porterfield
    Renewed the struggle at the ford ;
    And at the moment when the sword
Swayed in the balance where to yield,
    In middle of the mad melée
    Young Ugo snatched his flag away,
Leapt from the hot, opposing shore,
    The banner tied about his waist,
And in the flood plunged fiercely o'er,
    By a hundred whistling bullets chased,
And soon, with wild ecstatic hand,
He waved it mid our shouting band.

Naught dearer fills a soldier's sight,
Or swells his breast with more delight,
Than when his flag, late scorned and shamed,
Is by some comrade's hand reclaimed.

Another look, the ford was clear,
The foe was reeling to the rear ;
And now the smoke came deeper on,
And Nora from our sight was gone.

But still her voice rang high and loud :
　The speaker hid, the sound so near,
It seemed some spirit of the cloud
　Spake those prophetic words of fear :—
'Too late ! too late !' this was the cry :
'Fly, Ringbolt, Ugo, comrades !—fly !
　The reinforcing foe is here !'

What followed then I scarcely know,
　Save that we dashed amid the smoke,
And where we saw a red line glow,
　There fell our fiery battle-stroke :
Like a mad billow of the main
　We broke upon those thundering banks,
Then, drawing backward, formed again,
　To burst anew along their ranks.

For hours the scene was still the same,—
A sleet of lead mid sheets of flame ;
The hot hail round us hissed and roared,
Through clouds of seething sulphur poured,
　Until—we knew not how or why—
The day was lost !　Our saddened view
Between the smoke-wreaths' opening wrack
Beheld the patriots falling back :
　The hour of victory had gone by !

Still fighting, we our line withdrew,
    Scorning to yield or fly.

And now we gained a sheltering wood,
    Where, (oh, it was a sight to whet
    The sword of vengeance keener yet!)
Pale with the streaming loss of blood,
    By hireling foemen still beset,
Beside his foaming charger stood
    The wounded, gallant Lafayette.

We swept between, with scathing blow,
    Until his bleeding wound was bound:
Each drop of his the cloven foe
    Paid double to the crimson ground,
Until from off that field forlorn
The noblest son of France was borne.

But, oh, the sight, the last and worst,
That now upon my vision burst!—
I saw, beyond a thicket-screen,
Pale Nora o'er a warrior lean:
His head upon her knee she nursed,
    And held unto his fainting lip
    The can he scarce had strength to sip.
A few swift leaps, we gained the place.

Oh, be the hireling doubly cursed
　　Who caused that noble breast to groan !
It was my father's upturned face
　　Which looked into my own.

' Nay, son,' he faintly sighed, the while
His features wore a struggling smile,
' Be not dismayed, 'twill pass anon :
　　'Tis but a little loss of blood :
I am content : my hand has done
　　On many a foeman work as good ;
And some, methinks, will never tell
Beneath what old man's sword they fell.
But bear me hence : this trifling wound——'
Then in my circling arms he swooned.
Nay, start not : still it was not death,—
His breast anon recalled his breath.

We made a couch of fallen boughs,
　　Which thickly strewed the woodland path,
　　Torn by the cannon's flying wrath,
And, with such speed as pain allows,
Conveyed him to the cavern, where
He rests in Nora's watchful care ;
Then, with the moon to light my way,
I rode to tell how went the day."

V.

THE BATTLE IN THE CLOUD.

THE red October by his tent
  Sits painted in his warrior-hues;
Beside him lies, in peace unbent,
  The bow which he too soon will use.

O'er all the hill-sides near and far
  He sees the wigwam-smoke dispread;
There all his waiting warriors are,
  Streaked with their many tints of red.

Through all the realm of elm and oak
  The blue wreaths of their pipes increase:
Alas! the calumets they smoke
  Are not the sacred pipes of peace!

They plan around their council-fire
   The ambush on to-morrow's track;
They do but wait their warrior-sire
   To give the signal of attack.

The smile upon his lip to-day,
   The dream-light in his plotting eye,
Are but prophetic signs to say
   How fierce the arrow-storm shall fly.

Thus Esther mused, as from her tower
   She gazed o'er misty stream and land:
She knew 'twas but War's breathing-hour
Ere he again, in all his power,
   Should wave his flashing battle-brand.

Even there, beneath her very gaze,
   The invader's bristling lines were spread,
Wrapt in the calm October haze,
   And, like the Indian autumn, red.
From Delaware their scarlet ranks
Reached even to the Schuylkill banks,
So near the very mansion-wall
Echoed the frequent bugle-call,—
A sight to make her young heart sad,
   And all her patriot hopes destroy,—

While Berkley's loyal breast was mad
　　With uncontrolléd bursts of joy.

He gave the invaders every proof
　　How much his wishes with them lay:
Their flag was waving on his roof,
　　His halls received them night and day;
He even broached his buried store,
　　And brought a dozen hampers out,
Willing with generous hand to pour,
　　Repaid by loyal song and shout.

But one there was whose bowing plume
　　Was chiefly welcome to Sir Hugh,
And once before that banquet-room
　　Had felt his presence through and through,—
The same who on that long-gone night
　　The maiden's swelling song had heard,
Who deigned from his great warrior height
　　To stoop, and own his heart was stirred.

Now oft in Berkley's ear apart
　　He spoke about the maiden's hand:
"The heiress of such noble land,
Sir Hugh, should have a noble heart."

And once, with condescending lips,
He bowed and kissed her finger-tips,—
Sufficient such approving sign
From colonel of the royal line.

Thus passed a few calm days away;
   And now the night was not yet gone,
   Its dreamy veil but half withdrawn,
Fair Esther on her white couch lay,
Her soft light melting through the shade;
Her cheek against her hand was laid,
Round which the dainty flaxen curls
Were cast in little golden whirls,
As Love's own toying fingers light
Had twirled them o'er the pillow white.

That rounded arm, that angel face,
   The breast that stirred the snowy frills,
The whole light form of perfect grace,
Which the soft covering seemed to trace
As loving it with warm embrace,—
   All this the conjuring fancy thrills;
Thrills with a sense of sweet restraint,
As when before some sculptured saint,
Or lovely vision poured in paint

By some pure master, when his heart
Was molten with the fire of art.

Across her face strange shadows played,
As if by struggling pinions made;
For she was dreaming of the fray,
   Watching, amid the smoke-wreaths dun,
   Her Edgar bravely battling on,
The fiercest hero of the day.
She saw him riding midst the din
That raged around the Warren Inn,
And on Paoli's fearful plain,
   When Massacre the sword had drawn.
The trumpet's near and startling strain,
   That fiercely shook the cloudy dawn,
The drums that rolled their loud alarms,
And legions springing up to arms,
Flashed through her dream, and, when she woke,
Upon her ear the tumult broke!

Leaders were hurrying to and fro,
Proclaiming far, "The foe! the foe!"
"The foe! the foe!" rang over all,
And woke the echoes of Berkley Hall.

When Esther looked from her casement high,
Fear trembling in her large blue eye,
She stared against the vapor dank
Of morning hanging gray and blank.[7]

Great wrestling voices in the cloud,
Made by the mist more clear and loud,
Appalled her ear; the sudden roar
Of swift artillery shook the shore;
While here and there the half-blurred flash
Burned, and every window-sash
Answered to the thunder-crash.

Anon she saw some warrior-form,
Like the great genii of the storm,
Rise into shadowy giant height,
And then another of equal might,
And now the followers swung in sight,
Wielding great arms,—as oak with oak
Were battling in the hill-side smoke;
Or armies of the infernal god,
With lightning and with thunder shod,
Were wielding their gigantic blades
Against the crests of kindred shades;
Or, rather, as some pale, strange light
Were shining on some unseen fight,

And these the shadows fierce and tall
It threw upon a cold gray wall,
Struggling in many a rise and fall.

A scene of horror clear descried
  Must make the stoutest spirit quail;
But horrors doubly magnified
Behind a half-concealing veil
May well make maiden's cheek grow pale.

She watched the sun rise o'er the field,
A great disk like a bloody shield,
And 'gainst it rose a vision dim,
Made clearer by that burning rim,
Two plunging riders huge and grim;
Their fiery chargers seemed to swim
  Together in the wild commotion,
  Like war-barks in a roaring ocean.
But who is he, that warrior slim,
  Now lost to sight, and now more plain?
The agile form proclaims it him
  The object of her heart's devotion.
But, see!—oh, monstrous!—even the sun
Burns redder, beholding three to one,—
Three striking and one parrying! Now,
  Doubling the tumult of the scene,

Another giant swings between!
Swift flash the blades around his brow,
Like lightning o'er some rocky crest,
Drawn by the metal in its breast:
But, like the storm-defying rock,
Harmless about him breaks the shock;
The battle-clouds, confused and rent,
Are backward hurled, their thunders spent.

Still side by side the heroes fight,
Following the foe from left to right;
Swift flies the Wagoner's whirling blade,
And Edgar's is its very shade.

See how they rear, and plunge, and smite,
And, fighting still, wheel out of sight.
Her throbbing eyes can bear no more:
She sinks, half fainting, to the floor.

But no! her heart is with the cause:
  Shall she thus sink away dismayed
  The while her Edgar's flaming blade
  Is flashing even as she bade?
One deep, renewing breath she draws;
  She scorns the weakness thus displayed,

14

Contemns the soul that now would pause,
   And gains her feet, no more afraid.

         .

Before his door, with sword in hand,
Sir Hugh was making warlike stand,
When a troop of loyalists came by,
Uncertain if to fight or fly:
Such contradictory news was tossed
   Through fogs that veiled the battle-din,
   They dared not say which side would win,
   But to their secret hearts within
They owned the dreadful day was lost.

One glance at Berkley Hall they threw,
And saw the flag which o'er it flew :
" Ho, sirrah rebel ! who are you?"
They cried, and trooped around Sir Hugh.
" Rebel !" he echoed, in disdain :
" Who dares such words apply again,
This hand shall drive the lying breath
Back to his throat through bleeding teeth ;
This sword shall cleave the caitiff through
Who dares that insult to renew."

" Ho ! ho !" they cried,—" a prize ! a prize !
   The rebel dog, through fear and shame,

Would skulk beneath a loyal name;
But where yon rag insults the skies
  We know full well our right to claim."

" That rag? Insult?"—He choked with ire;
He said no more; his eye of fire
Flashed confidently o'er the roof,
When—oh, the staggering, deadly proof!—
His heart, as from a towering crag,
  Fell back, as stunned in dismal plight.
  Where now his valiant soul of might,
The spirit never known to lag?
There, sailing on the winds aloof,
  He saw the hated patriot flag,
While Ugo's clear and ringing voice
  Flung from the watch-tower far and free—
Making the misty air rejoice—
  The fiery shout of Victory.

Bold Berkley stood with wonder dumb,
  Confused, as dead to sight and sound;
But, when he felt his senses come,
  He chafed to find his arms were bound;
And then, with high, indignant mien,
Mounted two surly guards between,
He left with threatening brow the scene.

Sir Hugh long cursed the fatal hour
Which saw that flag upon his tower:
Oh, sad mischance that placed it there
In that wild moment when despair
Was trembling down the royal line,—
　　When Victory, with her thrusting hand,
Through blinding fogs, strove to consign
　　Her laurel to the patriot band![8]
And Berkley, ready for the field,
　　At his own door, with waving sword,
Stood threatening with defiant word
　　The loyal troop which bade him yield.
And, further, his accusers knew
That members of the obnoxious crew
At all hours, day and night, had been
Prowling round Berkley Manor seen.

All these were ominous proofs and black
Which gathered on his troubled track:
No word of his could move the shade
Upon his loyal honor laid.

Some favor still the doubt received:
　　They would not touch his land or hall;
　　His daughter might retain them all.
This but in part his pain relieved:

His fancy saw marauding bands
Insult his house, o'errun his lands:
His daughter, too,—might she not be
Subject to rough brutality ?

His fears were vain : his mansion through,
  When the withdrawing troop went down
  To hold their quarter in the town,
Was guarded better than he knew.

VI

HEAD-QUARTERS.   .

O'ER town and cottage, vale and height,
Down came the Winter, fierce and white,
And shuddering wildly, as distraught
At horrors his own hand had wrought.

IIis child, the young Year, newly born,
   Cheerless, cowering, and affrighted,
Wailed with a shivering voice forlorn,
   As on a frozen heath benighted.
In vain the hearths were set aglow,
   In vain the evening lamps were lighted,
To cheer the dreary realm of snow :
Old Winter's brow would not be smoothed,
Nor the young Year's wailing soothed.

How sad the wretch at morn or eve
Compelled his starving home to leave,
Who, plunged breast-deep from drift to drift,
Toils slowly on from rift to rift,
Still hearing in his aching ear
The cry his fancy whispers near,
Of little ones who weep for bread
Within an ill-provided shed!

But wilder, fiercer, sadder still,
  Freezing the tear it caused to start,
Was the inevitable chill
  Which pierced a nation's agued heart,—
A nation with its naked breast
Against the frozen barriers prest,
Heaving its tedious way and slow
Through shifting gulfs and drifts of woe,
Where every blast that whistled by
Was bitter with its children's cry.

Such was the winter's awful sight
For many a dreary day and night,
What time our country's hope forlorn,
Of every needed comfort shorn,
Lay housed within a hurried tent,
Where every keen blast found a rent,

And oft the snow was seen to sift
Along the floor its piling drift,
Or, mocking·the scant blankets' fold,
Across the night-couch frequent rolled;
Where every path by a soldier beat,
   Or every track where a sentinel stood,
Still held the print of naked feet,
   And oft the crimson stains of blood;
Where Famine held her spectral court,
   And joined by all her fierce allies:
She ever loved a camp or fort
   Beleaguered by the wintry skies,—
But chiefly when Disease is by,
To sink the frame and dim the eye,
Until, with seeking forehead bent,
   In martial garments cold and damp,
Pale Death patrols from tent to tent,
   To count the charnels of the camp.

Such was the winter that prevailed
   Within the crowded, frozen gorge;
Such were the horrors that assailed
   The patriot band at Valley Forge.

It was a midnight storm of woes
   To clear the sky for Freedom's morn;

And such must ever be the throes
  The hour when Liberty is born.

The chieftain, by his evening lamp,
Whose flame scarce cheered the hazy damp,
Sat toiling o'er some giant plan,
  With maps and charts before him spread,
Beholding in his warrior scan
  The paths which through the future led.

But oft his eye was filmed and dim,
  And oft his aching bosom yearned,
  As through the camp his fancy turned
And saw sad eyes which bent on him
  The look which they in pain had learned.
The sunken orbs of hunger there,
  With those that throbbed in fever-rage,
  As he their suffering might assuage,
Turned on him their imploring stare.
And when he spoke the kindly word
Oft from his lips of pity heard,
  And saw those eyes grow bright the while
  They caught the courage of his smile,
His sorrowing heart was doubly stirred.

And, to relieve his burdened breast,
His face into his hands he prest,
And poured his secret soul in prayer,
Where hope still rose above despair.

And there was seated by his side
  The noblest of a noble line:
  Her whole soul in her face benign,
Through love and suffering purified,
Shone worthy such a chieftain's bride.

And not alone his prayer was given,—
She joined him in imploring Heaven:
Those prayers fell not in barren sands
  Beside Oblivion's fruitless sea,
But, borne aloft by angel hands,
  They bloomed to flowers of victory.

The eve was late: naught met the ear,
But tramp of sentinel marching near,
Or soft and feathery beat of snow
  Blown light against the window-pane,
To melt thereon, and tearlike flow,
As if the sympathetic glow
  Within had turned each flake to rain.

At times there came the slumbrous sound
 Of waters toiling at the mill,
Still singing, though in fetters bound,
 The song learned on their natal hill.
 Let Winter, with oppressive will,
Bind down the stream with chains of ice,
His utmost power shall not suffice
 To keep that heart of Freedom still:
Though prisoned in the frozen pond,
 It only reinforcement waits
 To burst the tyrant's heavy gates
And leap to liberty beyond.

Thus with the tranquil flood of power
 Within that camp of ice and snow;
 Though all was silent outward show,
They did but wait the opening hour.

The night was late: the chieftain heard
 Approaching footsteps up the yard;
A knock: he rose, and gave the word:
 The door swung wide; the snowy guard
Announced, with some unwonted stir,
An unexpected visitor,
 With two attendants there beside.
It was a maid with cloak of fur,

And hood, so closely round her tied
That well the storm had been defied.
So thick the snow was o'er her blown,
  So flaxen was the falling braid
  Beside the rosy cheek displayed,
  She looked like some fair Norland maid
Wrapped in a robe of eider-down.

Beside her stood a youth whose mien
  Brought to the chief's remembering eye
The stripling hero he had seen
  Bearing a banner proudly high,
Within a light-horse flying line,
That fearful day at Brandywine.
The other was that sturdy dame
  The housekeeper: you saw it all
In one glance at that stately frame,
  Queen of the keys of Berkley Hall.

The maid a moment seemed to stand
  Abashed before that presence high:
  He read it in her timid eye,
And took in his her trembling hand.
She felt her young blood swifter run;
  Her heart could not regain its calm;

Her little hand lay in his palm,—
The noble palm of Washington!

Then rose the lady, with serene,
Sweet looks o'er all her stately mien;
    And she too took her hand, and spoke
In winning accents low and mild:—
"It is a stormy night, my child,
For one so young to be abroad;—
Or have you wandered from your road?
    Pray, loose your snowy hood and cloak,
And warm you well beside the fire,
And take the rest which you require.
Shrink not because the place is small:
Our hearts, we trust, have room for all."

When Esther answered, "Noble friends,
    We have not wandered from our way,
    Nor need we now for warmth delay;
Our glowing purpose freely sends
Its heat, and we would straightway do
The duty Heaven directs us to.

Much have we heard of all the ills
Suffered along these winter hills,—

15

Of famine in the frozen camp,
Of cheerless couches, cold and damp,
Where sickness breathes its painful breath
Mid bitter wants that usher Death.

Hence have we come, with courage armed,
With every deep compassion warmed,
To do the little in our power
To soothe the suffering of the hour.
Our sleigh is standing at the door,
Laden with such poor, hasty store
As one home from its winter hoard
Can to a bleeding cause afford:
And now it but remains to ask
Permission to assume our task."

She ceased, and stood with glowing cheek,—
So beautiful, so young and meek,
She seemed an answer to their prayer,—
A very pitying angel there.
    The chieftain's eye grew dim with mist,
His heart was all too full to speak;
The lady's arm the maiden prest,
She drew her to her matron breast
    And tenderly her forehead kissed.

The chief put out his hands, and smiled,—
   He laid them on her golden hair,
   And said, in feeling words of prayer,
"God bless you, noble child!"

VII.

THE WINTER CAMP.

'TWAS midnight in the soldier's shed,
Where lay upon his burning bed
The sufferer, to whose fever-glow
Most welcome came the gusts of snow,
On searching night-winds, icy thin,
Through every cranny blowing in,
Filling the place with frequent mist,
That round the one poor taper hissed.

Close at his side an aged man
Sat, like a good Samaritan,
Pouring the sacred oil and balm,
His pains and spirit-wounds to calm.
A cloth about his brow was bound,
To shield a deep and stubborn wound,

While round his neck the intruding air
Lifted and fanned his thin gray hair.
Across his knees his warrior sword
Sustained the book o'er which he pored:
The leaves were yellow, old, and stained,
   And oft by fluttering, rude winds stirred,
But still his aged eyesight strained
   To read the sacred, unstained Word.

But who was she who knelt beside,
   And held the sick man's hand in hers,
   Feeling such pain as only stirs
The breast where love and truth abide?
It needs but one glance to suffice
To know those large and dewy eyes;
But keener sight 'twould take, I ween,
To recognize that altered mien
Of him whose features scarcely prove
The Edgar of her hope and love.

   But saddest of her painful lot
To look into those eyes which burned,
To find no answering look returned,—
Those eyes whose gladness ever flew
In love to hers, with pleasure new :—
   Alas! alas! he knew her not!

A moment thus in prayers and tears
Her bosom poured its flood of fears;
But, conscious that, though blind with pain,
    His heart was hers, and hers alone,
She summoned strength, and stood again
    Strong in his love and in her own.
As one who on a battle-plain,
Feeling his life-blood dew the ground,
Seizes the scarf which love had bound
With trembling hands his breast around,
And thrusts it in the bleeding wound
To staunch the crimson tide of life,
Then springs anew to join the strife,
To give, perchance, the fatal blow
Which lays the invading foeman low,—
So rose the maid, and firmly prest
His love into her bleeding breast,
And strove, with all such hands can do,
To win him back to health anew.

It was a charmèd sight to see
    How lovingly she came and went,—
How like a sunbeam, silently,
    She cheered and warmed that winter tent.
Her cloak of fur around the wall
    She hung, to intercept the blast;

Across the door was spread her shawl,
    And every cranny was made fast.

Nor here alone her care was given:
    She daily passed from shed to shed;
The early morn, the noon, the even,
    Still found her near some sufferer's bed.
And striving oft, as she had striven,
    There praying mid the sick and dead,
    She saw the chieftain's bowing head,
    And heard his word of courage said:
    Where'er they smiled there seemed to spread
The soft and healing breath of Heaven.

Not fruitless was her constant care,
And not unheard her daily prayer:
The blackest cloud of all was past;
    New sunshine filled the winter skies;
Hope came to Edgar's couch at last:
    No more her face his glance denies;
    His soul responded through his eyes
    With all the warmth which love supplies.

And with the first returning breath—
    A breath as sweet as that which stirs
        Through April boughs, when all the woods

Feel the first thrill of promised buds—
He owned his soul was doubly hers,
Since she had called it back from death.

One day, as by the scanty fire
She strove to make it sparkle higher,
   The while her patient's slender form
   Was propt beside, and mantled warm,
The old man, Edgar's patriot sire,
Entered with overshadowed brow,
   And said, "Sweet daughter, come with me ·
I fear another couch may now
   Lay claim to your fidelity.
The strange wild woman you so oft
   Encountered in your winter round,
   And who so frequently you found
Soothing the sick with accents soft,—
Accents which suited not the dress,
So fitted for the wilderness,—
Now lies a victim to the spell
Which she in others strove to quell,
With fever sorely racked and thrilled,
Mid kindly hands, but all unskilled.

I have not yet forgot the day
When on the battle-field I lay

Almost in death, she was the first
To slake my fever-flame of thirst,
Or how within the secret cave
   She tended me so well and long,
Cheering me oft with some wild stave
   Of ballad or of mountain-song,
And oft, as though I were a child,
   (There's something in her brain amiss,)
Telling some legend strange and wild.
   For this—— But nay,—it needs not this
To wake compassion in your eyes :—
A human creature suffering lies."

Then Esther rose, and joined her guide,
   And reached the shed where Nora lay ;
But, when she stood by Nora's side,
   Her heart of courage sank away.
For, oh, it was a piteous sight
To see those eyes so strangely bright,
And all that flood of scattered hair
As blown by winds of wild despair,
And all the trappings of her dress
Flung wide by hands of hot distress !

There Ugo by the wagoner stood,
And both in anxious, gloomy mood ;

She stared upon the wondering child,
  Then wept as o'er some burning thought,
Then gazed at Ringbolt strangely wild,
  And laughed, as though her pain were naught.
The saddest of àll sounds that flow
Is laughter forced from deeps of woe.

A moment on the maid she glanced,
As if her spirit hung entranced,
And now, with curious, searching scan,
Surveyed the pitying, gray-haired man,
And spoke with low, mysterious air :—
" Thou poor young bride, beware! beware!
Oh, wed not with that cold white hair!
That summer smile is but device :—
His breast is snow, his heart is ice.
        Oh, cold was the bridegroom,
          All frozen with pride!—
        He first slew her lover,
          Then made her his bride.
Ringbolt, how goes the battle?   Ho!
Fly, Ugo!—fly! the foe!—the foe!
A stealthy trick!—but they shall know
The stricken can return the blow!
The tyrant and his host shall flee,—
When patriots strike, they shall be free!

Our flag like a meteor
  Sweeps down through the fight:
It brightens the valley
  And burns on the height.

Oh, did you not see
  How it sprung like a flame
When the voice of the nation
  Called Freedom by name?

On the soul of the tyrant
  That mighty name fell,
As in Gessler's heart quivered
  The arrow of Tell!"

Thus sang she, and fell back with breath
Drawn faint, as through the lips of death;
The life within the frame consumed
Seemed scarce again to be illumed.
Then Ringbolt gazed on her with eye
Of pain,—almost of agony,—
And said, with heavy, solemn tongue,
" 'Tis hard for one so good and young
To suffer thus! The poor white dove
Was murdered by a falcon's love!"

Then Esther said, "Indeed, my frien ls,
It is a sight which sadly sends
The blood back on the heart, to see
Such depths of human misery.
Oh, surely this wild, dismal camp
Is all too rough and cold and damp:
'Twere better if she were conveyed
And in some quiet chamber laid,
Mid hands that know to tend and spread
The comforts of a sufferer's bed,
Where pity only holds control,
With not a sound to vex the soul.
And such a room my heart allows,
Within a well-provided house,
And well I know her couch will find
The hands attendant, gentle, kind;
For Hulda, ever good and mild,
Will guard her as she were her child.
Haste, Ugo, haste, and bring the sleigh,
And let her be enwrapt straightway:
'Tis but a short two hours' ride;
So easily her course shall glide,
So deep shall be her bed of fur,
So soft and noiseless be the stir,
That she may sleep and never know
How swiftly fly the miles below."

A moment there was seen to go
  O'er Ringbolt's face a blackening cloud:
  At length his nodding forehead bowed:
" Perchance," he said, " 'twere better so."

The sleigh was brought, and many a fold
  Of fur and blanket wrapt her form;
And now within the wagoner's hold,
  Like a light infant, close and warm,
She lay,—and thus, beside the maid,
To Berkley Mansion was conveyed.

He bore her up the shadowy stair,
The wildered sufferer knew not where,
And in a chamber warm and large
He left her in kind Hulda's charge.

A cup of wine,—bluff words of thanks,—
  If Esther would regain the camp,
    Ugo must be her guard and guide,—
  The great hall heard his heavy tramp,
    The deep snow marked his giant stride,
Which led him up the Schuylkill banks
To join again his waiting ranks.

VIII.

THE HERALDS.

DAYS came and went round Nora's couch:
  If there was need of aught to tell
  That gentle hands attended well,
Her mild and altered mien could vouch.

Weeks came and went, and every day
  Brought better news from out the valley:
Each tiding-tongue was glad to say
  The troops, the cause, all seemed to rally.
And Esther's heart, though still her sire
  Was captive in the royal camp,
Saw Hope re-fan her smouldering fire
  Within the cloud's desponding damp.

'Twas evening, and she watched the gleam
Of moonlight over hill and stream ;
Though winter now was wellnigh through,
   And springtime promised soon to blow,
Still, all the scene which met her view
   Lay in a gleaming robe of snow.
She sat and gazed upon the stars,
   As on a banner there unfurled,
   And wondered if each sparkling world
Was shocked like this with martial jars,—
   If through those tranquil, silver skies
   Stern warriors bent devoted eyes
In worship on the planet Mars.

She mused,—when Hulda's waking hand
   Was laid upon her resting arm,
   And, looking up with mild alarm,
She saw within the moonlight stand
Another, whose brave feet had paced
Through paths of snow in breathless haste.

" I come"—this was her hurried word,
   She scarcely seemed for breath to pause—
" To you, for I have often heard
   Your heart is with our patriot cause :

You have swift horses at command,
And have, perchance, some trusty hand
 By whom a message may be borne:
The word I bear must reach our band
 Before to-morrow morn."

"Speak on!" the startled hearer cried:
"It shall, no matter what betide!"

"Our enemy a plan has laid—
 I got the news, it boots not how—
By which our camp shall be betrayed,
And all our noble army made
 To bite the dust, or basely bow.
This was their threat;—and even now
 Their rapid horsemen form in line,
 And ere the dawn 'tis their design
To strike the fatal blow.

This is the news: I pray you speed:
The hour is short, and dire the need:
 I have no time to answer more;
But if our noble chief would know
The source from which these tidings flow,
'Then tell him boldly, undeterred,

'Tis Lydia Darrach's faithful word,[9]
　Which served him once before."

"Thanks, noble heart!" young Esther cried,
And flung her daring tresses wide:
　"Spite every danger or mishap,
Ere yon low moon shall disappear,
The news shall reach our General's ear
　Though death stood in the gap!"

Waiting no more to hear or say,
The herald took her homeward way.

"Now, Ugo!"—this was Esther's call,—
"Bridle the swiftest steed in stall,
Fly with the news you just have heard,
And let our chieftain know the word."

"A steed!" he answered; "but suppose
The road should be beset with foes,
The boldest rider scarce would do
To bear such needful tidings through.
No, no: I have a better way,—
　One quite as swift, and far more sure;
Nor horse nor man my course shall stay,
　I shall be mounted so secure."

16*

She stared at him with puzzled brow,
　But he nor look nor answer stayed;
　She heard the rattling which he made
Within the dusky hall below;
She saw him dash across the snow,
　Until he gained the frozen river,
Watched him a moment bending low,
Then, like an arrow from the bow,
Beheld his flying figure go
　On skates, with many a flash and quiver,
As if the glistening ice and steel,
In lightning, would his speed reveal.

The smile applauded the device:
　She watched him, with a glad surprise,
　Until he vanished from her eyes.
　But suddenly, with fear renewed,
　She stood in anxious attitude:—
That messenger upon the ice,
It might, and yet might not, suffice.
If highways held the foeman wolf,
The river also had its gulf,
And 'twas the season when the sun
Old Winter's work had half undone;
The snowy eaves were thawed at noon,
The thinning ice must vanish soon;

The moon, too, hung with sinking disk;
　Her light would shortly be at end.
　No, no: it would not do to send
One messenger on such a risk:
All must be staked to win or lose;
In such a cause, who stayed to choose?

In haste she ordered out the sleigh:
None heard the maid her purpose say;
'Twas not for others' ears discussed,
For there was none whom she would trust,
Save Hulda, and her duty lay
Round suffering Nora night and day.
Alone she mounted, without pause,
To save, perchance, her country's cause:
Away, away, the light car flew;
　The hoofs flung up the powdery snow;
　Swift as a river seemed to flow
The road beneath, where, slipping through
The crispy foam with whistling shrieks,
The runners left their glistening streaks.

Oh, enviable star in heaven
That looked through that still crystal even,
And saw how those two heralds went,
Each on the same high mission bent,—

One on a road of ice below,
One on a streamlike road of snow,
The locks of each flung backward far,
And trailing like a meteor star:
Oh, ne'er before sped soul with soul
In holier race for earthly goal!

Just as the last hill-top was neared,
    And the swift horses slackened pace,
    A voice, as if it broke through space,
Pealed to the welkin as it cheered,
Announcing the last danger cleared :—
'Twas Ugo's wild, triumphant mirth,
Ringing as it would circle earth.

And thus the two young heralds met,
In spite of foes about them set,
    In spite of dark and wintry weather,
And to the grateful patriot chief,
In burning language plain and brief,
    Delivered their great news together;
And soon the horses, flecked with foam,
Well pleased, were turned again for home.
While Ugo took the guiding rein,
Thus held the maid her musing vein :—

" Now the moon has left her track,
   Dropt behind the mountain-bars ;
   Paly shine the cold white stars,
And the pale earth answers back ;
All the world a shadow lies,
   Darkly, breathless, deathly still,
While above us hang the skies,
Throbbing to our throbbing eyes,
Till the fancy almost hears
   Something of the strains that thrill,
Passing through the happy spheres.

Yonder the great Northern Wain
Rings across the azure plain,
   Nightly rolling toward the goal
   Of the ever-steadfast Pole :
   Every steed in that great car
   On his forehead wears a star,
Proud with bells upon his mane.

Sweetest of the chimes of heaven
Is yon clustered sister-seven,
In their turret's misty height,
Like a stem of lilies white,—
Our sweet valley Pleiades,
Ringing perfume on the breeze.

Ring, sweet sisters, clearer still:
My heart listens for the thrill
From your sacred belfrey-cell:
Pour your chime; but, ah, the knell
Floats from off your silver lips
For that lost one in eclipse!

Lost!—ah, no: she is not lost;
 Her song was too fine and sweet
 With your singing to compete;
On some more celestial coast
She is now the angels' boast,
With her joy forever told,
In a tower of shining gold.

Ring, sweet stars of heaven, anew,
And my heart will sing with you;
Ring!—oh, ring!—that I may hear
And feel that heaven is sometimes near."

Thus Esther in her happy breast
The pleasure of her soul confest;
For she was glowing with a sense
 (Although the thought had scarcely heed)
 That she had done a sacred deed
Which was its own sweet recompense.

The singing sleigh, the horses' tread,
  Slow pacing homeward at their will,
The flowing road that backward sped,
The stars that chased her overhead,
  Like heavenly guardians with her still,
  The crystal air, but not too chill,
All soothed her with a gentle calm,
As if a cool and tender palm
Were on her tranquil forehead prest
To woo her into peaceful rest.

And Ugo held in dreamy spell
  The reins which seemed about to fall;
But homeward steeds remember well
  The road which leads them to their stall.

All nature seemed as it were fanned
  With Slumber's cool and downy pinions;
But, hold!—the steeds are at full stand!
  Around them close the foeman's minions!
Is she awake, or does she dream?
  The sword-flash that before her stirs,
The scarlet coat, the helmet's gleam,
  The bursting laugh of rude derision,
  A rough voice shouting, "Prisoners!"

A soldier at each horse's rein,
And Ugo dragged among the train,—
    All this proclaims it is no vision.
The boy is loud,—he will not stay :
A boy is he, armed soldiers they.
" What men are ye," she strove to say,
" Who dare to stop a lady's way ?
    I charge ye, off !   Unbind the boy !"
Whereat the captain's voice replied,
Close at the startled maiden's side,
    " Lady, we wish not to annoy
Further than strictest duty calls :
Be not alarmed : if aught befalls
Amiss, the fault shall not be ours,—
We serve the cause of higher powers :
Though it seem hard, and you condemn,
Our prisoner, you must go to them."

He took the reins, and said no more :
    With mounted men to guard them down,
Even past her own unhappy door
    She went a captive to the town.

PART III.

17

THE TANKARD OF WINE.

Oh, what delight is in the air
What time the new-born spring is there !
How sweet it is on the breezy slope,
Mid flowers in bloom or about to ope,
When the dog-wood, like a maiden dight
In bridal robes of snowy white,
Beside the flaming maple stands,
While the oak, with priestly hands
Spread above their bowing heads,
His whispering benediction sheds;
Where never a careless wind forgets
To tell of the woodland violets,
Or how it half forgot to pass
From spice-wood boughs and sassafras;

195

And, like the soul of a mocking-bird,
Repeating every song it heard,
Each sweeter for being brought afar,
As all the joys of memory are.

Such Esther knew were the delights
Clothing the valley and the heights;
And every perfumed air she met,
   Fresh breathing of the wood and field,
Filled her with longings and regret
   For joys the city could not yield.

Had she a pleasure in her breast,
In secret it was all suppressed;
For every look and every tone
Proclaimed her Melancholy's own.

'Twas true, her captive chains were light,—
Another might have deemed them bright;
But, light or bright, she felt the pain
Of knowing that there was a chain
Which flowers, though twined with subtlest art,
Could not make welcome to her heart:
They could but hide from others' stare
The galling weight she knew was there.

The city and its farthest street
Were free to her unfettered feet;
But there was still that line beyond,
O'er which her feelings, wildly fond,
Took yearning wing, and well she knew
She could not follow where they flew.

Sir Hugh grew daily more appeased:
  He mingled with the martial court,
  His fetters seemed but things of sport,
And even now might be released
If he in any slight degree
Would bow and sue for liberty.
But no! they had assailed his pride:
His loyalty had been denied:
He would not bow the suppliant limb,—
Nay, rather they must bow to him.
And now, too, all he held most dear
Next to his pride, his child, was here,
And many a noble officer
Bowed supplely low to him and her;
And even those with hearts allied
In secret to the patriot side
Made him obeisance; for they deemed
He might be other than he seemed.

These flattering tributes to him paid
Gave sweet contentment, and he stayed.

———————

'Twas twilight, and the evening air
Came dancing over Delaware,
Fanning the easy sailor's hair,
Who laughed and quaffed away his care,
With merry song and gusty din,
Under the stoop before the inn,
Where soon, arrayed in colors fine,
Two officers of the royal line
Reeled singing in at the open door,
    Aflush with pleasure and with wine :
'Twas noble, they said,—or rather swore,—
    With such a general to dine.

Each face was scarlet as their dress :
    The whole man seemed to loom and shine,
    As if the red blood of the vine
Its glowing presence would express
    By every visible outward sign.

" Ho, landlord of the 'Ship and Sheaf,'
Bring us a flagon, and be brief !

We must not let the tide go by,
To leave us stranded high and dry,
Or wait to-morrow's evening flood
To lift us o'er the sand and mud;
'Twill never do to stick aground
While other barks are sailing round:
Let loose the wine, and, should that fail,
Then swim us off with good brown ale!"

Thus shouted they, then searched the gloom,
To note what guests were in the room:
Their glance found only two beside.
" Two fellows there I think I spied,"
Thus whispered one.   " Nay, there are more,"
The other answered,—" surely four:
    But two, perchance, are made of wine!"
Whereat they laughed; and still they swore
    'Twas noble, glorious, and divine
    With such a general to dine.

" Ho, landlord, bring another flask,
To nerve us for to-morrow's task!
To-morrow's task!   Ah, that will be
A scene of such rare chivalry
That all shall go joy-mad to see!—

A thousand times more bright and fine
Than Germantown or Brandywine!
How those poor devils in the gorge,
Hidden away at Valley Forge,
In their tatterdemalion rags,
Making their empty rebel brags,
Would ope their boorish eyes to gaze
Upon the splendors which shall blaze
And burn, until the night is spent,
Around our glorious tournament!
Come, landlord, drink, before we go,
A bumper to the royal show!

That fellow there, who seems to sulk
And in the shadowy corner skulk,
Go bring him out, and let him clear
His throat, that he may loudly cheer
The golden glories he shall see
Around to-morrow's pageantry!
Come, sirrah, when a colonel bids,
Nor sit with scowl like pirate Kidd's:
This wine will smooth your hostler frown
When it washes the hay-dust down!"

The stranger rose: through a sideway door
He pushed a young companion out,

Then stood a moment as in doubt,
The while he scanned the revellers o'er,
Then strode to the table with visage grim,
Demanding what they would with him.

"To drink our general's health!" they cried.
"Our general!" boldly he replied,
  And drained the goblet willingly.
"And to our tournament beside!"
  "And to the tournament!" echoed he;
  "And may I be on hand to see!"

"Again!" the other cried, with zest;
"Fill high!—methinks that were a breast
To hold a gallon in its chest,—
And let the toast be to the fair,—
To her whose colors I shall wear,—
The badge of the 'Burning Mountain' mine,
'The maid I love' my motto sign.
Then pledge for whom I set the lance,
With whom in banquet I shall dance,—
Perchance"—he hiccoughed, and waved his wine—
"To her who may be bride of mine,—
I have the father's word for all:
  Or, if not that"—with drunken leer
  He whispered in his comrade's ear,

Then laughed till the cup was nigh to fall,
And shouted, " The heiress of Berkley Hall!"

The stranger's tankard was ready up;
    Each his lip was about to dash,
    When, with an oath like a thunder-crash,
    He flashed the wine in the speaker's face
And into the other's the empty cup,
    And then, with heavy, giant pace,
    Strode leisurely beyond the place;
    And, ere they woke from their disgrace,
A light boat and a springing oar
Had borne the wagoner far from shore.

II.

THE MESCHIANZA.[10]

O CITY the beloved of Penn,
How was your quiet startled when
Red Mars made your calm harbor glow
With all the splendors he can show!

How looked your tranquil founder down
That day upon his cherished town,—
That town which in the sylvan wild
He reared and tended like a child?

Methinks that patriarch and his peers,
  Who fashioned all your staid retreats,
  Groaned then in their celestial seats
With sad offended eyes and ears;

And, had their loving faith allowed,
That day, in mournful spirit bowed,
Each had turned his olive-wand
Into a rod of reprimand.

The May was there,—the blue-eyed May;
The sweet south breeze came up the bay,
Fanning the river where it lay
Voiceless, with astonished stare,—
The great sea-drinking Delaware.

There, in the broad, clear afternoon,
With myriad oars, and all in tune,
   A swarm of barges moved away,
  In all their grand regatta pride,
As bright as in a blue lagune,
When gondolas from shore to shore
Swam round the golden Bucentaur
   On a Venetian holiday,
  What time the Doge threw in the tide
  The ring which made the sea his bride.

Mid these were mighty platforms drawn,
Each crowded like a festal lawn,—
Great swimming floors, o'er which were rolled
Cloth of scarlet, green, and gold,

Like tropic isles of flowery light
Unmoored by some enchanter's might,
O'erflowed with music, floated down
Before the wharf-assembled town.

A thousand rowers rocked and sung,
A thousand light oars flashed and flung
A fairy rainbow where they sprung.
Conjoining with the singers' voice,
 In ecstatic rival trial,
Every instrument of choice,
 Mellow flute and silver vial,
Wooed the soft air to rejoice;
Till on wings of splendor met,
Clearer, louder, wilder yet,
Clarion and clarionet,
And the bugle's sailing tone,
As from lips of tempests blown,
Made the whole wide sky its own,
Shivering with its festal jar
The aerial dome afar.

Thus the music past the town
Winged the swimming pageant down,
Till with one loud crash it dropt,
And the bright flotilla stopt,

18

Mooring in the bannered port
At the flowery wharves of Sport.

There wide triumphal arches flamed
With painted trophies, which proclaimed,
With mottoes wrought in many a line
Around some brave heraldic sign,
That all the splendors here displayed
Were honors to great chieftains paid.

Pavilions round the field were spread,
With flying banners overhead,
Where, on a high and central throne,
The two commanders reigned alone:
The admiral, whose powdered hair
Had oft been fanned by ocean air;
The general, whose eye oft sped
O'er fields transfused from green to red,
As if the very plain should wear
The hue his army held so dear,—
Both deeming that the world must bow
Before the awful name of Howe.

And there,—oh, feast for painter's heart,
And yet a light to mock his art,

To kindle all a poet's fire,
To waken, madden, and inspire,
Yet leave him mastered and undone,
As faints a taper in the sun,—
Yes, there, in many a beaming row,
Was lit such beauty as might glow
Alone in fabled tourney-rings
   Held in those far enchanted scenes
   Where all are princesses and queens
And all the jousting knights are kings.

Such light was then our city's boast;
And such, methinks, it has not lost:
The features Stuart loved to trace
   And clothe in his immortal glow
Are met by many a soul-lit face,
Secured by Sully's touch of grace,
   As bright as theirs of long ago.

O noble masters, might I here
   Seize the light pencil from your grasp,
Then should the picture reappear
   Which vainly I attempt to clasp.
What though the vision with me stays,
The awkward pencil tamely strays,

And leaves me, after all my cost,
To sigh above my labor lost.
But ye who have the conjuring will,
   The painter's gift, the poet's heart,
Take the rough lines I cannot fill,
   And touch them with your clearer art.

In middle of the central group—
The fairest maidens of the troop,
Each in her flowing Turkish dress—
Sat Esther, in her loveliness.
A graceful turban bound her brow,
Its end flung back in gauzy flow,
And from its sides hung loops of pearls,
Dripping among the golden curls,
While on its snowy front was set
A diamond stellar coronet,
And in the middle of the stars
A red rose shone, like burning Mars;
The silken robe, of ample fold,
Was white, and bound with belt of gold,
O'er which a scarf of wondrous lace
Added its wealth of flowing grace.

Her beauty thrilled the gazing crowd,
   And made the heart of Berkley glad;

But if Sir Hugh that hour was proud,
　Still prouder was the stripling lad,
Brave Ugo, who beside her chair,
　With height and form beyond his age,
　Stood near, her guardian and her page;
His large dark eyes and raven hair
To hers made contrast rich and rare;
And, decked in Oriental suit,
He looked a Turk from head to foot,
Holding superb and tranquil mien,
As by the throne of a sceptred queen.

Now rang the bugle to the cloud;
　And now seven knights, in brave attire
　　Of white and scarlet gayly donned,
　　On chargers well caparisoned,
　And each attended by his squire,
Rode in before the admiring crowd;
　And soft eyes sparkled brightly fond,
As each before his lady bowed.
　Then rang the herald's trumpet higher,
And swelled the challenge fiercely loud:—
　　" The brave knights of ' The Blended Rose'
　　　Proclaim the fair whom they defend
　Are lovelier, nobler in their pride,
Than all the world can show beside;

And he who dares this vaunt oppose
   We challenge to the direful end!"

Three times abroad the vaunt was thrown;
And now another bugle blown,
Flinging its scorn around the heaven,
   Ushered in the answering troop,—
The gallant and defying seven,
In suits of orange and of black,
With harnessed steeds and squires to back;
   And these with proud and knightly stoop
Made their obeisance to the fair
Whose beauty they defended there.

Then swelled the other herald's cry :—
" ' The Knights of the Burning Mount' defy,
And, in support of their ladies' charms,
Challenge all chivalry to arms!"

But how looked Esther on the scene?
   Was there no pleasure in the place,
   To call the color to her face?
A weary sadness veiled her mien;
Her eye, which took the splendor in,
Mid all the show no joy could win;

For in her patriotic heart
Another picture, far apart,
Rose, with its drear, contrasted shade,
　Before her sympathetic eye,
　　Which glistened with a pitying damp.
　　She saw the starving valley camp,
　And heard the sufferer's dying sigh,—
Saw all the bitter wants that weighed—
　Her country's only hope and trust—
　A noble army to the dust;
And even when her champion proud
　Bent low, a gallant knight in black,
She scarcely noticed that he bowed;
　Her sad eye paid no glances back.

Again the flying bugle's flash
　Across the waiting scene was pealed;
Then came the sudden shock and dash
Of spears that met in splintering crash
　On every loudly-ringing shield.
Then sword with sword together rang
With many a fierce and fiery clang,
　As on some earnest battle-field.

Oh for the pen which brave Froissart
　Waved, sword-like, in the knightly van!

Oh for the pencil and the art
  Of battle-loving Wouverman !
That on my page might be unrolled
Another tourney " cloth of gold" !

All eyes were on the struggle bent,
And every gazer forward leant,
Each breathless at the whirling sight,—
When dashed in midst another knight,
Driving the raging foes between,
And, like a whirlwind, joined the scene.

His tall and foaming steed was black,
  And reared and leapt with plunge and wheel;
And he who loomed upon his back
  Wore on his breast a plate of steel,
While on his head a helmet shone
With flying plume,—the visor down.
The armor was embossed and rich,
  And seemed to Esther to recall
The helmet and the breastplate which
Formed part of that within the niche,—
  The ancestral suit of Berkley Hall;
  As if the knight, so grim and tall,
  Finding the ancient form too small,

Content to shield his head and breast,
Had borrowed but cuirass and crest.

His raining blows were swift and bold:
  No sooner was his weapon set
  'Gainst every lifted blade he met,
Than flew that blade from out its hold;
While many a bravest knight, alarmed,
Recoiled apace, abashed, disarmed.

But when he met the searched-for foe,
  Fair Esther's champion in the list,
  His mighty hand could not resist,—
He dealt an angry, giant's blow,—
Perchance it was intended so;
Somehow, the awkward weapon missed,—
  It glanced beyond the approaching head,
  And on the "black knight's" mouth instead
Alit the great hilt-clenching fist!
A blow that made the earth swim round,
And sent him bleeding to the ground.

Then, while the murmur questioned loud,
He dashed to the wondering maid and bowed,
And raised her white glove to his lip.
  Now seemed her eye to understand;

She guessed that form of high command,
And felt a folded paper slip
　　Stealthily into her startled hand;
Then, like an eagle on flashing wing,
He sailed beyond the wondering ring.

All marvelled; but few guessed the truth:
　　They mostly thought it in the play;
And even the knights, with frowns uncouth,
And many a savage inward oath,
　　Were pleased among themselves to say
That some hot-headed frolic youth
　　　Had chosen thus to share the day,
　　　By dashing in the jousting fray,
　　　To bear the highest prize away,
　　　And leave them all in wondering doubt,
　　　As oft in ancient tourney-bout.

The two commanders, looking on,
Approved the novel action done,
And said, in accents loud and bluff,
　·　　The brave surprise was well performed,
　　　And that it was a knightly thing,
Although, perchance, a little rough.
　　　And catching this, as from a king,　·
　　　The shout of joy ran round the ring,

Till every clapping hand was warmed,
   To send the applause on circling wing.
And now the day was wellnigh spent,
And evening closed the tournament.

III.

THE BANQUET.

OH, merry and good is a blooming wood
　　On a calm, clear afternoon,
When every maid, in a flowery hood,
Sings, as every maiden should
　　In the leafy shades of June :—
When every light form wears the proof
Of what beneath her homestead roof
　　The loom of Winter weaves,—
The blue, and green, and scarlet woof,
　　The white and flowing sleeves :—
When every archer bends his bow,
To bid the laughing arrow go
　　Among the laughing leaves !

And merry the call to a Christmas hall,
　　Where nuts and ale abound,

Where music, with gusty rise and fall,
Chases the revellers dancing all
  In many a mazy round.

But louder, clearer, merrier yet
The music and mirth together met
What time the evening feast was set
  And the tournament was through:
The knights came in, each waving plume
Sending a murmur through the room,
And, bowing to eyes they deemed most sweet,
Each knelt before his lady's feet,
  To receive the trophy due.

But where was Esther's champion?
Had he no tourney-honor won?
  And must the flower her turban wore
Remain unclaimed, and feel the blight
Of all that withering festal light?
She plucked the rose with fingers white,
And tore the leaves before their sight
  And strewed them on the floor.

That feasting-hall was a sight to see,
And, seen, it must remembered be:

A hundred banners lined the wall,
   Festooning over swords and spears,
   And thrice a score of chandeliers
Made such a glory through the hall
   As only summer noonday wears;
And many a mirror, wide and tall,
   Decked with flowers on golden piers,
Caught the splendor, and echoed it all,
As if to stretch the gorgeous place
Into the outer halls of space,
   As it were to last a thousand years.

All, all was bright as summer waves
   That sing and dance on a flowery shore,
Where the billow decks the bank it laves
   With pearls, and then retreats for more.
   The only shadows around the feast
Were a score of turbaned, Nubian slaves
   Arrayed in livery of the East.

The merriest sounds o'erflowed the scene,
While flashed the brimming wine between,
Where each, from the cup he loved to quaff,
Caught something of its vineyard laugh.

There was whispered love, soft words of bliss
On lips Adonis would die to kiss,
   Rustle of silks, and rattle of fans,
Tinkling of glasses, and, crowning this,
   Music that swelled from invisible clans :—
Till, closing his eyes, the listener heard
   The rush of a woodland waterfall,
And all the leaves of the forest stirred
   By a flutter of wings, and the noisy call
Of every loudest-throated bird.

The feast was past, the toast was said,
The inevitable speeches made,
And the long-cheered, triumphant two
Breathed easier, and drank anew.

'Twas now that one of the leading knights
   Bowed, and, with soft persuasion long,
Prayed, as a wreath to their delights,
   Our maid would crown the hour with song.

In vain her timid lips demurred :
The praise of her voice so much was heard,
They would not take the denying word.
In view of this, a harp had been,
Only a moment past, brought in.

And there in a flood of light it shone
Golden on its waiting throne.

At length, upon her father's arm,
  And bidding her page beside her stay,
She went, though tremorous with alarm,
  And André, bowing, led the way.
    She gained the throne, and sat thereon:
      Her breath came short for such a need;
One glance across the room she sent,
A thousand eyes were on her bent;
    They seemed a thousand arrows drawn,
      And she the victim that must bleed.

One long sustaining breath she drew,
Her drooping lids shut out the view,—
Till, suddenly dashing her veil aside,
And flinging her golden ringlets wide,
Her arms around the harp she pressed,
Loving it with her loving breast,
    As if its touch her fears might smother.
      And now her hands along the strings
    Flashed daringly across each other,
As when two birds, at dividing wires,
Outsinging all the woodland choirs,
      Flutter with half-invisible wings.

When climbed her fingers high and higher,
  Twinkling among the treble notes
  There seemed unnumbered silver throats,
Thrilling the sky with wild desire;
Then sudden lightnings flashed their fire,
Till, in the heavier chords below,
The thunder dealt its rumbling blow;
And now the rain was shivered down,
And all the tempest-bugles blown.

Then came her voice: at first 'twas low,
  Like a sweet brook among the rushes;
But, like that brook, its further flow
  Swelled soon to fuller, nobler gushes.

SONG.

I.

In the vanished time and olden,
Ere the ages yet were golden,
A great king ruled his misty isles
  In sullen state alone,
  Till, hearing of a maiden
  With marvellous beauty laden,
He swore she must be brought to him
  To tend beside his throne.
19*

II.

And forthwith every vassal
Who dwelt beside his castle
Was sent to bring the maiden in
    Before the morrow morn;
And straightway to her bower
They went in all their power:
But she met them with her noble mien
    And scorned them with her scorn.'

III.

"Go, tell your tyrant master
Earth threatens no disaster
So direful to a maiden's soul
    As is a monarch's smile;
That Death shall wed me rather
'Neath the roof-tree of my father,
Than I should serve the greatest king
    That ever ruled an isle."

IV.

Then laughed they loud derision
At the poor defenceless vision
Of a simple maid who dared alone
    Defy their mighty king;

"Then come," they cried, "the trial;
Our lord brooks no denial:
Your slender wrists must bear the bands
Our master bade us bring."

V.

But, firm in her reliance,
With a glance of fierce defiance
She looked into their cowering eyes,
That drooped as in disgrace!
But, remembering royal anger,
With a sudden clash and clangor
They drew their mighty falchions forth
And flashed them in her face.

VI.

A moment, as in sadness,
She looked upon their madness,
With calm, white arms serenely there
Upon her bosom laid;
Then, with no thrill of terror,
But smiling at their error,
Three times she clapped her snowy hands,
And signalled thus for aid.

VII.

Three times her palms resounded,
And at once she stood surrounded
By noble brothers rushing in
From every native field:
Their forms were rough and tawny,
But their limbs were lithe and brawny,
And, instead of taking captors there,
The captors now must yield.

VIII.

And, against their own consenting,
She sent them back repenting.
The mad king cropt their coward ears
To satisfy his wrath:
And still that noble maiden,
With all her beauty laden,
Went singing on her happy way,
With honor in her path.

Scarce had the last word left her tongue,
And while the chord still trembling hung
From which the bird-like note had sprung,

There rose a tumult wild without,[11]
A hurried rush of loud alarms,
The flash of flames, the sentinel's shout,
  With startled drums that beat to arms.
The shuddering guests no more could doubt,
But quaked to think the rebel crew
  Had burst in all their midnight power
  Upon them, in their revel hour,
To act the Trenton scene anew.

What meant that glow whose fearful shine
Illumined the abatis-line,
Which fired the scene, as if to light
The horrors of the coming fight?

Now could they hear the mounted troop
Like hungry vultures round them swoop,
And see the clattering hoofs of steel
Where lightning flashed from every heel.

Out rushed the guardian ranks aflame,
To put the intruding crew to shame;
But, strange to tell, without a blow,
To say that there had been the foe,
The troopers fled, and left behind
Their mocking laughter on the wind.

The guards pursued them past the town,
By the same road which brought them down,
And soon the sentinels descried
The line returning, flushed with pride.

Then laughter filled the hall again,
While pleasure took the place of pain,
And every happy face was lit
With this fresh source of mirth and wit,
And music spread its circling wing
To lead the dance in ampler swing.

But what was wrong?   What ailed Sir Hugh?
Why sought he thus the assembly through?
What were the questions he would pour
At every outward-leading door?
At last he stood, with sigh long drawn,—
Both Ugo and the maid were gone.

One said that while the guardian troop
    Had gone to beat the rebels back,
He saw descend a hasty group
    Across the lawn, and some were black,—
A part of that same turbaned horde
Who tended while the wine was poured,—

And that they moved towards a bark :—
   To shield them, then, the white moon bowed
   Behind a heavy wall of cloud :—
He saw no more, for all was dark.

IV.

THE BROTHERS.

WHAT light illumes the eagle's ken,
  And flames his breast with Freedom's rage,
The first wild daring instant when
  He soars beyond his broken cage!

How glows the lion's eye of fire,
Brighter than lit with midnight ire,
The moment when he sees the bar
Half drawn that leaves the door ajar!
How proudly he exalts his mane
That first hour on the open plain!

When from the winter's captive hold
  The young spring takes the freedom won,

While all his fetters crystal cold
   Melt like a vision in the sun :—

Then every river, brook, and rill
Feels its deep heart with pleasure thrill;
Then sing the birds, and every tree
Waves its gay hands for jollity.

What joy, my own dear land, was thine,
   What pleasure filled thy breast of sorrow,
As if the heart were pulsing wine,—
What glorious sunshine filled the noon
That cloudless, jubilant day in June
   Which said, "The foe will leave to-morrow!"

"To-morrow!" every glad eye-glance
To that sweet music seemed to dance:
Youth spread the shout from first to last,
   And Age new vigor seemed to borrow,
And stranger-faces, as they passed,
   Looked that masonic word, "To-morrow!"

The happy country heard afar
   The answer of its long desires;
     Swift sped the news from hill to hill,
     O'er plain and valley wandering still,

20

As if on every mountain-bar
  Was lit the flame of signal-fires.

And there were eyes in Berkley Hall,
  That, bright before, were now more bright,—
Young breasts that in their rise and fall
  Were thrilled with uncontrolled delight.
Yet there beneath the Berkley roof
Were looks that angered at the proof,—
Dark, sullen brows, which seemed to say
The morn would bring a hateful day.
'Twas hard to see the old reins slip
From out their doting monarch's grip;
And so, to nerve them for the worst,
  The purple flask must cheer the hour,
That they at least might slake their thirst
  For wine, if not for tyrant power.

" To-morrow, Colonel, you depart :"
  This was the greeting of Sir Hugh.
" Believe me when I say my heart
  Is sad to part with such as you.
I hoped ere this—but hopes are vain :
    There is a higher Wisdom rules :—
Though wise his ways, they are not plain :
    'Tis strange, and yet He sometimes deigns

To give an empire's guiding reins
   Into the hardy hands of fools :—
I hoped ere this—that hope at least
   Holds good, and shall not be denied—
To see my family-board increased,
   To see my daughter at your side
   A lovely and contented bride.

How stands your glass?   The room is dim :
   Methinks the twilight settles soon,
   In spite of the long days of June ;
   And yonder rises the red moon,
As if wine flushed her golden brim.
So flush your glass ; for wine, in truth,
   Which sparkles in these founts of ours,
Is that perpetual Spring of Youth
Which Ponce de Leon strove, forsooth,
   To find within the land of flowers.
Then never let our spirits sink,
   Though Time and Fate their worst pursue,
While at the bacchanalian brink
   Our hearts their courage may renew.

Ay, courage,—'tis the soldier's word :
   The hour is brighter than it seems ;

To-day, even while you stood deterred,
   I caught from hope some clearer gleams.

Did you not notice, when we came,
   And after my first warm embrace,
How flushed her cheek and eye with flame
   When she looked up and saw your face?
I felt her little wild heart leap,
   That moment, in my clasping hand;
For Love, when he would safely keep
His head in secret hiding deep,
   Is but an ostrich in the sand.

What though her look no hope awakes,
   Repelling with disdainful eye,
'Tis but the course the salmon takes,
   In scornful distance pausing shy;
Just when you think your toil is vain,
And when he chiefly shows disdain,
   With sudden whirl he takes the fly!
What though her mien conceals the spell,
Believe me, friend, she loves you well.

Who spoke?   Who dared to give the lie?
   Ho, Steward! lights!"

The lights were brought,
And every secret hiding-place
Was peered into with angry face.
   The furious searching furnished naught
To meet his pistol's ready rage,
Except a parrot in his cage :
Yes, surely 'twas that silly bird
Who uttered the obnoxious word.
They laughed, and sat : the wine must serve
To smooth again the ruffled nerve.

" To prove, my friend, my words sincere,
I have the paper ready here."
Thus spake Sir Hugh. " It only waits
For the contracting names and dates :
'Tis quickly done. There, mine secures
The seal ; and now, my friend, for yours.
By Jove ! your pen flies o'er the word
With all the flourish of a sword !

The maiden's name ? Ah, never doubt :
   That with the rest shall soon appear.
Ho, Steward, seek your mistress out
   And bid her to attend me here !"

In Berkley's breast resolve was stern,
   For in his proud parental heart,
   Remembering with what willing art
   Her favor took the patriots' part,
He felt a deep resentment burn.
   Although he loved her fondly still,
Yet, though all else should be denied,
   She should not set her rebel will
Against this last hope of his pride:
It may be that the flush of wine
Gave vigor to his fixed design.
Young Esther came: her eye was bright
As if 'twere brimmed with love's own light;
Then flowed her maiden accents clear,
"What would you, father? I am here."

"A trifling service," he replied;—
   There was a strangeness in the tone
   Which turned her inmost heart to stone:—
"Before these written names are dried,
Let yours be drying at their side."

With wondering countenance advanced,
Her eye across the paper glanced;
Her visage showed a lightning-blight,—
   The color from her cheek was blown,

As when from off some festal height
   The fierce bolt strikes the banner down.

Before her flashed the ready quill,
   The black blood waiting at the point;
Across her swept a deathly chill
   That agued every sinking joint:
A very statue, mute and white,
She stood, till came the order, "Write!"

"Nay, father: any thing but this,—
   If 'twere to die at your command!"
He answered, "My sole order is
   To write! The pen is in your hand!"

'Twas there; for he had placed it there,—
   He seized her by the slender wrist.—
"Oh, help!" she cried.

                  "Nay, to assist
In your rebellion who shall dare?"
He answered firmly, at the word,
Tapping his pistol and his sword.

Her hand was on the paper prest:
   Both watched it with their anxious ken;

The blood was curdling in her breast,
　A deadly pallor veiled her mien,
The room swam round in darkness,—when
　An iron hand was thrust between,
Which snatched and crushed the crackling pen !

Three paces back, with shuddering reel,
　All started, in their horror dumb ;
　Their tongues even as their hearts were numb ;
For there a voiceless form of steel
Stood glowering as with threatening will ;
For, though the visor close was down,
The very iron seemed to frown,
The clenching gauntlet grasping still
The crumpled remnant of the quill.
Within the waning light and gloom
To giant size it seemed to loom :
Such necromantic power has fright
To give to objects double height.

While now the gazers stood aghast,
　The form, with slow and backward pace,
　Confronting still with iron face,
Retiring, reached the throne at last
　Where stood the maiden's harp of gold.

Still paler grew the lights and dim,—
Or so the frighted fancy told,—
While phantom lustre seemed to swim
About that form so ghostly grim;
And, just behind, the moon's broad rim
Seemed to the very casement rolled,
A spectral chariot waiting him:
The gazers' blood ran doubly cold
And palsied every limb.

But stranger still it was to see
The form slow sinking on one knee,
Upon the harp's enthroning stand,
While in his stretching arms he took
The frame, whose chords in terror shook
Ere scarce they felt the iron hand.

Slow o'er the strings the gauntlets stole:—
(That gloves of steel showed little skill
In answering to the player's will,
Such audience would scarcely wonder;)—
But, with a strange, weird music still,
That wailed above, then rumbled under,
He played as 'twere a funeral dole
Chanted by distant winds and thunder;

And when from out the helmet broke
   The words in many a dying close,
It seemed as if a cavern spoke
   The burden of long-hidden woes.

SONG.

I.

A shade has crossed the hill, Sir Hugh,
   A shade has crossed the lawn ;
And where its phantom feet have gone,
So lightly were they pressed thereon,
They did not brush the evening dew,
            Sir Hugh,
      They did not brush the dew.

II.

A gloom is on your house, Sir Hugh,
   Your sire frowns on the wall,—
Where frown those painted shadows all,
Now pale and shuddering o'er your fall:
The last of all the name are you,
            Sir Hugh,
      The last of all are you.

III.

Your royal cause is lost, Sir Hugh;
  Your king recoils aghast;
His day of tyrant power is past:
Of all his friends you are the last,
Last of your cause and name are you,
      Sir Hugh,
  The last of all are you.

IV.

The last of all are you, Sir Hugh,
  Echoes the owl aloof,—
The last of all,—upon the roof
The whippoorwill prolongs the proof:—
Adieu to Berkley Hall,—adieu,
      Sir Hugh,
  To Berkley Hall adieu.

"Behold! Sir Hugh, be not dismayed!"
The suitor cried, and drew his blade.
"Do you not see it is the same
Who boldly to our tourney came
A rough, unbidden guest and foe?
I have not yet forgiven the blow:

Though it were years, in twice the gloom
I still would know that helm and plume."

Through Berkley's brain the lightning sped,
  And, casting round his glances quick,
    Sir Hugh the empty niche espied;
    Then, with an angry laugh, he cried,
  "A trick! By Heaven! a rebel trick!"
And scarcely had the words been said,
  The room was blinded with a flash:
The iron vision forward sprung,
And reeled the frighted group among;
  And now the floor received the crash
Of one who falls in armor dead.
  Alas! if there was aught within
But ghost, to brave that bolt of lead,
  That shining breastplate was too thin!

The door, by sudden fury thrust,
  Swung wide, and hurrying men strode in,
And one, whose voice was like a gust,
  Cried, "Wherefore all this murderous din?"
Then, following Sir Hugh's wild stare,
He saw the fallen armor there,
And saw from out the iron seam
A mortal tide of crimson stream.

With hurried stride he crossed the floor,
And knelt beside the pool of gore,
   With rapid hand the visor threw,
   And started backward at the view:
One look told all,—no need of more:—
   From out its sheath his weapon flew.

"Behold," he cried, "O wretch, behold
   The murderous work your hand has done!
Ay, stare upon that visage cold,
   And recognize, mad fool, your son!
But, while there's strength within this hand
And steel of vengeance in this brand,
Your heart shall pour a stream as good,
Even though I shed a brother's blood!"

That moment he had forward sprung,
But Esther on his right arm flung
Her form, and there she pleading clung.

Then stood Sir Hugh as one who seems
Chained amid horrid nightmare-dreams;
Though fain to fly the sight of gore,
His feet were frozen to the floor.

At length he stammered, still with stare
Fixed on the pallid visage there,
" A lie!—a lie I I had no son,
And surely never such a one !"

To which the other cried again,
 " Thy son, proud fool, and son of her
Whose noble heart by you was slain,—
 O cold and double murderer !"

Still staring with unmoving eye,
He said,—or rather seemed to sigh,—
" I never killed her: if she died,
It was not here——"
                    " Your bitter pride
Struck at her heart, until her brain
By many a cold, proud word was slain !"
The wagoner answered; and the taunt
 At last awoke the Berkley blood.

" Who dares," he cried, in furious mood,
" Thus in my face such words to flaunt ?
And who art thou, who ne'er before
 Save once, a rude, unwelcome guest,
Was known to enter at my door ?

What rebel thou, whose coward breast
   Dares breathe the insult uttered now !"

" Pray, not so fast," the other cried.
   " A moment clear your clouded brow,
   And let your memory allow
I am not one to be defied !
That picture there may well attest
Whose courage ever was the best,
And which it was who quaked with fear
The moment danger came too near.
I scorned you even as a child,
   Proud, cold, and selfish as you were;
A younger brother, oft reviled,
   I would not be your pensioner,
And so I left you to yourself,
With all your boasted pride and pelf.

" A rebel !—nay, let that foul name
Flush your own coward cheek with shame:
'Tis ye are black Rebellion's knaves,
   Traitors to Freedom and to God,
   Who dare upon this sacred sod
   Exalt the slave-compelling rod,
Being slaves yourselves, to make us slaves !

While throbs a heart,—while Heaven is just,—
While on the banner of our trust
   One star remains to fight beneath,
   No blade of ours shall seek its sheath,
   No cannon hold its direful breath,
   Till on the bitter field of death
The bold enslaver bites the dust.
Already, even as pictured there,
   The joy has oft been mine to take
   In this good grasp the tyrant snake
And fling him writhing in despair."

"*My* brother, thou?" Sir Hugh replied,
The while the wagoner's form he eyed,
Scanning in scorn, from head to foot,
The patriot's rough and rustic suit.
" 'Tis false!   No Berkley scion yet
His high-born lineage could forget,
   To wear such rude and menial form
     And be the thing which thou art now!"—
He spake, and back recoiled a pace
Before the anger of that face:
   He dared no further brook the storm
     Which gathered on that threatening brow.
But now his troubled eye again
Was cast upon the stripling slain,

And, with a look which strove in vain
To hide the doubt within his brain,
He cried, " 'Tis false!   No blood of mine
  E'er wandered vagrant through the land;
  No Berkley son would raise a hand
In honor of the rebel line!
No child of mine——"

                His speech was stayed;
He glared upon the trembling maid.
" Well mayst thou tremble!" he resumed,
" And sink with burning shame consumed,
Whose recreant heart and rebel eye
Now give our loyal blood the lie!
'Tis thou, with disobedience long,
  This sad and direful scene hast wrought,—
  Firing the youth with rebel thought
And filling his soul with rebel song;
But that shall end!"   And, at the word,
Across the harp he flashed his sword
And severed every trembling chord.

" Strike on!"—this was the wagoner's taunt:—
" Such courage ever was your vaunt:
With no more stripling sons to kill,
On other innocents wreak your fill!"

"Still must I hear?" Sir Hugh replied,
"Are my assertions all denied?
The boy was never son of mine,
   Though harbored long beneath my roof:
In shades condemned, or realms divine,
That truant woman's wandering ghost
No Berkley offspring dares to boast:—
   I challenge every proof!"

The wagoner turned, and whispered, "Hark!
What newer misery thrills the dark?
What voice is that approaching near?
Sir Hugh!—Sir Hugh!—look up and hear!"

Thus as he spoke, a mournful air
Seemed winding down the shadowy stair,
Still nearing and more near; and soon
The words came clearly with the tune.

SONG.

I.

Oh, cold was the bridegroom,
   All frozen with pride:
He first slew her lover,
   Then made her his bride.

II.

Beneath a green willow,
  And under a stone,
They buried her lover,
  And left her alone.

III.

With naught but the bridegroom's
  Proud breast for her head,
Oh, how could she live when
  Her lover was dead?

IV.

Her body they buried
  Beside the church-wall;
Her ghost with the bridegroom
  Sat up in the hall:—

V.

Sat up at his table,
  Lay down in his bed:—
Oh, cold was the bridegroom,—
  But colder the dead!

The singer entered.   Was it a ghost,
   Or sleeper walking unaware?
Her large eyes, as in revery lost,
   Bent forward their unearthly stare;
   Wild o'er her shoulders fell her hair;
Her face was like her garments white;
Her thin hands bore a wavering light,
Which shed a pale and mournful glare
Across those features of despair.

Still forward walked that form of awe,
As if her wide eyes nothing saw,
Until, in middle of the room,
The centre of that scene of gloom,
She cast a slow, dull glance around,
And looked as she had nothing found:
Across their very faces past
   Those eyes to which all seemed a blank,
Till on the floor her glance was cast;
And there, as that look was her last,
She gazed upon those features white;
From out her fingers dropt the light,
   And on the armored breast she sank.

It needed but that last wild gust
   Of grief to blow from Nora's frame

Life's low, unsteady, flickering flame,
And leave it dark and soulless dust.

"Sir Hugh!—Sir Hugh!"   He was not there:
Sir Hugh was gone, they knew not where.

But there the haughty suitor stood,
  His bright sword flashing in his hand,
  As if the keen, defying brand
His nuptial claim should still make good.
This saw the wagoner, as he laid
On Edgar's arm the fainting maid;
And, ere the soldier was aware,
He stood without a weapon there:
His sword was in the patriot's hold,
  Who with a look of scorn surveyed
The face so lately flushed and bold;
Then, with contemptuous movement fleet,
  Across his knee he snapped the blade,
And flung it at the wearer's feet,
  And now, the wide door pointing through,
Exclaimed, with sad but threatening brow,
  "Depart!   The place is sacred now:
  Go, follow thou Sir Hugh!"

CONCLUSION.

My friend abruptly closed the book: -
  I felt as one who long had sailed
Gazing with anxious landward look,—
  Who, just as the fair port is hailed,
And the rough prow goes dipping in,
Suddenly hears the anchor's din,
And, lo! the ship is at full stand:
There move the people on the land,
And there are voices from the beach,
But mournfully all out of reach.

My face the crowding questions wore:
  He said, "A little patience yet,
And soon the landing skiff and oar
  Your feet upon the shore shall set."
Then at the sinking fire his hands
Gathered and piled the sundered brands,

Until the hearth was re-illumed:—
  "'Tis thus," he said, "the story stands:—
  A fallen end or two demands
To be regathered and consumed.

How goes the wine? 'Tis rare and old:
Or do you taste the earthy mould?
Some seasons past, while men of mine
  Were hollowing out an ample space
  To give our hothouse-wall its base,
  I stood to watch them bravely delve
And see they followed well the line,
  When suddenly to its very helve
The pick went in with crush and crash,
Spattering all with a purple splash;
And when withdrawn—oh, murderous sign!—
'Twas bathed in the streaming blood of wine.
How it came there to you is plain,
And this brings up Sir Hugh again.
'Tis said that on that night of pain
He rushed into the moonlit air,
And sped for hours he knew not where,
Through fields and woods, by the river's brim,
With two sad phantoms following him;—
How once, just as he thought he saw
The crowning horror of his awe,

The murdered stripling in his path
Rise with confronting eyes of wrath,
He reeled and staggered, fainted, fell,
And lay at the feet of a sentinel;
And when he awoke, and the horrid mists
    From off his aching brow were blown,
    He found himself within the town,
Among the guards of the royalists.

He recognized the hand of Fate;
    And, after writing a hurried scrawl,
    Giving his daughter Berkley Hall[12]
And his blessing with the broad estate,
He boarded a ship, and felt more free
    While bidding adieu to river and bay;
    But his heart was withering day by day,
And at last they buried him far at sea.

The lovers? Ah, more sweet the lay
    Should be which sings of those so dear:
It is not long since, old and gray,
    My sainted parents passed from here.

If 'twere not that the fire is low,
And chanticleer awakes to throw
    His midnight signal on the air,

A sacred scene should newly glow
  Of that beloved and loving pair.

My mother's favorite seat was there,
And this my father's high-backed chair:
How clearly comes the long-gone scene
When I a child sat here between!

One night,—I well recall the hour,—
  Just when our second war was past,
The winds were howling o'er the tower,
    The snow its gulfy deluge poured,
  And up the chimney like a blast
  · The flame from off the hickory roared,
Against the outer door a blow
  Sounded like a blacksmith's sledge,
  And, waiting no further privilege,
Entered, it seemed, the Prince of Snow,—
A veteran of giant height,
With wild locks like his garments white.
The heavy stamping and the beat,
  Which piled a drift within the hall,
  Rang through the house, and wakened all
The echoes to announce his feet.
So thick the cloud he scattered wide,
  And so majestic was the fling,

He seemed a very arctic king
Throwing his furry robe aside.

My sire, awakened by the stir,
   Gazed through the door with shaded eyes,
   Puzzled a moment with vague surprise;
   But when he saw that giant size
   And heard the voice of bluff replies,
He knew and welcomed the Wagoner.

Had you beheld him stride the floor,
You ne'er had guessed how many a score
Of years had blown their changeful air
Through those wild locks to whiten there.

We offered him this cushioned seat:
   He took yon great oak chair instead,—
   It felt more saddle-like, he said,—
And flung him down with wide-spread feet.

" 'Tis seventy years," he cried, " or more,
   Since first I backed a good, stout steed;
   And though to-day with as fearless speed
I rode as in the days of yore,
I know that wild, free course is o'er.

It boots not to prolong the strife:
That brave, old-fashioned, cheery life
Is ended.   My contented grip
  Resigns at last the guiding reins:
  No more my bells o'er hills and plains
  Shall ring, as once, through these domains.
And therefore I have brought my whip,
  To hang it up in Berkley Hall,
  To see it grace yon antlers tall
  Which hold those old swords on the wall,
The rusty weapons of Sir Hugh:
The honor is its well-earned due."

We welcomed him with hearty will,
And wished him many bright years still,
Then brought the wine—we knew the sort—
And brimmed a goblet with old port.
Through the red cup he gazed a while,
In musing, with a strange, sad smile.

"Good Uncle Ralph," my mother sighed,
  Dropping the embroidery in her lap,
"One question I have often tried
  To solve; and yet, through some mishap,
It seems conjecture wandered wide:

But you, I think, can solve for me
Poor Nora's mournful history."

The old man looked at her a space,
Looked vaguely in her upturned face,
As if endeavoring to recall
  The far scenes of the past, and said,—
" For her sake you should know it all,
  For my sake too, when I am dead;
But first, my friends, let me make clear
The reason I to-night am here.

Beside the old churchyard to-day
The surly sexton crossed my way :
He glared at me with sidelong leer,
  And flung his spade across the wall.
Just then a hurrying team drew near :
  The horses, wagon, bells, and all
(Believe me, 'twas a marvellous sign)
Seemed like the very ghosts of mine;
The driver—for once I held my breath,
        To see the flash
        Of his maniac lash—
Was a rattling skeleton, grim and tall;
His shout was the hollow shout of Death !

My team, with many a plunge and rear,
Went mad, then stood like frighted deer,
　While I sat like a girl aghast,
　Until that awful wagoner passed;
And when I looked behind, 'twas gone,
And we were in the road alone.

Think not that superstitious fright
Could cheat my ear or mock my sight;
Although the calendar counts me old,
My heart is as the youngest bold.
Brave Percy, when his charger stood
　First on the field of Brandywine,[13]
Beheld, in clear, prophetic mood,
The spot which should receive his blood;
　He saw his form's distinct outline
Stretched on the sod,—his steed, in fright,
Dashing riderless through the fight;
Then instantly he galloped on,
And sought the fate he could not shun.

It is a bitter night; the cold
For the first time now makes me old:
Another cup of this warm wine
　Perchance will give the blood a start,

And thaw the chill about my heart,
And clear this hazy brain of mine."

Again his vague eye scanned the glass,
As if he saw old memories pass
    In many a long and wavering line;
And, as he held the glowing cup
Between him and the lamp-light up,
The color of the deep wine threw
Across his face a purple hue:
I could but shudder where I stood,
It looked so like a dash of blood.

At last he spoke in under-tone,—
" Those grand old times are past and gone;
But, Esther,"—here his eye grew bright
With something of its former light,—
" Do you remember how of old
Around our cause your numbers rolled?
    I ever loved a fiery song;
But there was something in your voice
Which made the listener's heart rejoice,
His eye of courage burn more bright,
And filled him with a fierce delight
    That did not to the words belong:

To hear again such music sung
Would make a veteran heart grow young."

My mother's cheek turned somewhat red
To hear the praise so bluffly said;
It seemed to bring the vanished days
What time her song was used to praise.
She looked, and smiled, and shook her head,
   And said her voice had lost its power,
Her singing summer-day had sped,
   And she was in her autumn bower;
The water of a spring-time brook
   Makes plenteous music through the land,
But surely 'twas an idle look
   Which sought it in October's sand;
Her harp, too, since that night of pain
Had never known its chords again.

But still within her secret breast
She thought to humor him were best:
What though her voice had somewhat failed,
His aged ear, so long assailed
   By Winter, could not be o'er nice,—
The sense so long inured to storm
Might deem the cadence still was warm,
   Nor note its chill of autumn ice:—

And thus, to please an old man's whim,
With folded hands, she sang to him.

SONG.

I.

When sailed our swift eagle
   O'er valley and highland,
The foe, like a sea-gull,
   Fled back to his island,—
Fled back to his king-land,
   His home in the ocean,—
The white cliffs of England,
   His pride and devotion.

II.

Now peace and contentment
   Fill cottage and manor;
No star of resentment
   Is lit on our banner.
Our cannon is sleeping
   The port-shadows under;
The spell in its keeping
   Let naught break asunder.

III.

The impotent taunt let
  Go by,—the wind brings it;
But not the red gauntlet,
  No matter who flings it.
Who palters and falters,
  Ne'er hearken his story,
But strike for your altars,
  For Freedom and Glory.

"Nay, never say," the old man cried,
"Your voice is like a brooklet dried;
But rather say 'tis filled again,
O'erflowing with the autumn rain.

It carries me back, both brain and heart,
  As if a gale swept o'er the scroll;
  I see the storied past unroll;
And now, methinks, I may impart
  Something of Nora and the child.

My memory is a restive colt,
  Stubborn at times, contrary, wild,
At the wrong moment apt to bolt;

But wine upon an old man's lip,
To such a steed, is spur and whip."

Then laughed he his accustomed laugh,
　That shook the glasses on the board,
And, with a long and breathless quaff,
　The wine across his lip was poured :
The goblet dropt from out his hold,
　And crashed to fragments on the floor ;
Slow sank his chin, slow drooped his lid,
His heavy hands beside him slid ;
　He slept,—ay, slept,—but breathed no more,
And left the story still untold.

As when some monarch of the trees,
　　Which held so long defiant state
　Against the lightning and the gale,
　　O'erborne at last by its own weight,
While laughing in the passing breeze,
　Falls prone in the astonished vale,—
So fell our grand old Hercules.

NOTES.

NOTES.

With horrid noise of horn and pan,
Had borne in mockery up and down
The noisiest Tory of the town.

"Among the disaffected in Philadelphia, Dr. K—— was pre-eminently ardent and rash.   An extremely zealous loyalist, and impetuous in his temper, he had given much umbrage to the Whigs, and, if I am not mistaken, he had been detected in some hostile machinations: hence he was deemed a proper subject for the fashionable punishment of tarring, feathering, and carting. He was seized at his own door by a party of militia, and, in an attempt to resist them, received a wound in his hand from a bayonet.   Being overpowered, he was placed in a cart provided for the purpose, and, amid a multitude of boys and idlers, paraded through the streets to the tune of the royal march.   I happened to be at the Coffee-House when the concourse arrived there.   They made a halt; when the doctor, foaming with rage and indigna-tion, without his hat, his wig dishevelled and bloody from his wounded hand, stood up in the cart and called for a bowl of punch.   It was quickly handed to him,—when so vehement was his thirst that he drained it of its contents before he took it from his lips. . . .

"It must be admitted, however, that the conduct of the populace was marked by a *lenity which peculiarly distinguished the cradle of our republicanism. Tar and feathers had been dispensed with,* and, excepting the injury he had received in his hand, *no sort of violence was offered by the mob to their victim.*"

Graydon's Memoirs of his Own Times.

Note 2.   Page 80.

Oh, would some sweet bird of the South
Might build in every cannon's mouth !

This part of the poem was written six years ago; consequently the passage was not suggested by the cannon which "Disunion" has since then pointed against the North.

Note 3.   Page 90.

And, lo, he met their wondering eyes
Complete in all a warrior's guise.

"In concluding his farewell sermon, he said that, in the language of Holy Writ, 'there was a time for all things,—a time to preach, and a time to pray,—but those times had passed away;' and then, in a voice that echoed like a trumpet-blast through the church, he said that 'there was a time to fight, and that time had now come.' Then, laying aside his sacerdotal gown, he stood before his flock in the full regimental dress of a Virginia colonel. He ordered the drums to be beaten at the church-door for recruits, and almost all his male audience capable of bearing arms joined his standard."

Lossing's Sketch of the Life of General Muhlenberg.

Note 4. Page 106.

He gained the river and the cave.

The cave referred to is not a creation of the fancy, but exists in the vicinity indicated, and is the scene of more than one romantic legend.

Note 5. Page 113.

I watched the long, long ranks go by.

" Washington, in order to encourage its friends and dishearten its enemies, marched with the whole army through the city down Front and up Chestnut Streets. Great pains were taken to make the display as imposing as possible. To give them something of a uniform appearance, they had sprigs of green in their hats. Washington rode at the head of his troops, attended by his numerous staff, with the Marquis Lafayette by his side. The long column of the army, broken into divisions and brigades, the pioneers with their axes, the squadrons of horse, the extended trains of artillery, the tramp of steed, the bray of trumpet and spirit-stirring sound of drum and fife,—all had an imposing effect on a peaceful city unused to the sight of marshalled armies. The disaffected, who had been taught to believe the American forces much less than they were in reality, were astonished as they gazed on the lengthening procession of a host which to their unpractised eyes appeared innumerable; while the Whigs, gaining fresh hope and animation from the sight, cheered the patriot squadrons as they passed." *Irving's Life of Washington.*

NOTE 6. PAGE 130.

The soft air felt the jar
Of thunder rolling from afar.

All the chronicles agree in stating that the cannonading at the battle of Brandywine was distinctly heard at Philadelphia and its vicinity.

NOTE 7. PAGE 155.

The vapor dank
Of morning hanging gray and blank.

A heavy fog enveloped Germantown on the morning of the battle, which, "together with the smoke of the cannon and musketry," says Irving, "made it almost as dark as night."

NOTE 8. PAGE 160.

When Victory, with her thrusting hand,
Through blinding fogs, strove to consign
Her laurel to the patriot band.

" Every account confirms the opinion I at first entertained,— that our troops retreated at the instant when victory was declaring herself in our favor. I can discover no other cause for not improving this happy opportunity than the extreme haziness of the weather."   *Washington to the President of Congress.*

Lydia Darrach's faithful word.

"*Mrs. Darrach's Conduct.*—I have very direct and certain evidence for saying that Mrs. Lydia Darrach, the wife of William Darrach (a teacher, dwelling in the house No. 177 South Second Street, corner of Little Dock Street), was the cause of saving Washington's army from great disaster while it lay at Whitemarsh in 1777. The case was this. The adjutant-general of the British army occupied a chamber in that house, and came there by night to read the orders and plan of General Howe's meditated attack. She overheard them when she was expected to have been asleep in bed; and, making a pretext to go out to Frankford for flour for family use, under a pass, she met with Colonel Craig (who afterwards shot himself) and communicated the whole to him, who immediately rode off to General Washington to put him on his guard. The next night, about midnight, the British army, in great force, marched silently out of Philadelphia. The whole affair terminated in what was called, I believe, the action of Edgehill, on the 5th of December; and, on the 8th following, the British got back to the city, fatigued and disappointed. Lydia Darrach and her husband were Friends. She communicated all the particulars (more than here expressed) to my friend Mrs. Hannah Haines, and others. Although she was a small and weakly woman, she walked the whole distance, going and coming, bringing with her—to save appearances—twenty-five pounds of flour, borne upon the arms all the way from Frankford. The adjutant-general afterwards came to her to inquire if it had been possible that any of her family could have been up to listen and convey intelligence, since the result had been so mysterious to him." *Watson's Annals.*

A similar stratagem was planned to surprise Washington at Valley Forge; but, the fact being communicated in time, the enemy was foiled by the sudden and unexpected appearance of Lafayette and his corps on the banks of the Schuylkill.

Note 10.   Page 203.

The Meschianza at Philadelphia.

"The Meschianza was chiefly a tilt and tournament, with other entertainments, as the term implies, and was given on Monday the 18th of May, 1778, at Wharton's country-seat, in Southwark, by the officers of General Howe's army, to that officer on his quitting the command to return to England.

"The company began to assemble at three to four o'clock, at Knight's Wharf, at the water's edge of Green Street, in the Northern Liberties; and by half-past four o'clock in the afternoon the whole were embarked, in the pleasant month of May, in a 'grand regatta' of three divisions.

"When arrived at the fort below the Swedes' Church, they formed a line through an avenue of grenadiers and light-horse in the rear. The company were thus conducted to a square lawn of one hundred and fifty yards on each side, and which was also lined with troops. This area formed the ground for a tilt or tournament. On the front seat of each pavilion were placed seven of the principal young ladies of the country, dressed in Turkish habits, and wearing in their turbans the articles which they intended to bestow on their several gallant knights. Soon the trumpets at a distance announced the approach of the seven white knights, habited in white and red silk and mounted on gray chargers richly caparisoned in similar colors. These were followed by their several esquires on foot. Besides these, there was a herald in his robe. These all made the circuit of the square, saluting the ladies as they passed, and then they ranged in line with their ladies; then their herald (Mr. Beaumont), after a flourish of trumpets, proclaimed their challenge in the name of 'the knights of the blended rose,'—declaring that the ladies of their order excel, in wit, beauty, and accomplishments, those of the whole world, and they are ready to enter the lists against any knights who will deny the same, according to the laws of ancient chivalry.

"At the third repetition of the challenge, a sound of trumpets announced the entrance of another herald with four trumpeters dressed in black and orange. The two heralds held a parley, when the black herald proceeded to proclaim his defiance in the name of 'the knights of the burning mountain.' Then retiring, there soon after entered 'the black knights,' with their esquires, preceded by their herald, on whose tunic was represented a mountain sending forth flames, and the motto, 'I burn forever!'

"These seven knights, like the former ones, rode round the lists and made their obeisance to the ladies, and then drew up, fronting the white knights; and, the chief of these having thrown down his gauntlet, the chief of the black knights directed his esquire to take it up. Then the knights received their lances from their esquires, fixed their shields on their left arms, and, making a general salute to each other by a movement of their lances, turned round to take their career, and, encountering in full gallop, shivered their spears. In the second and third encounter they discharged their pistols. In the fourth, they fought with their swords.

"From the garden they ascended a flight of steps covered with carpets, which led into a spacious hall, the panels of which were painted in imitation of Sienna marble, enclosing festoons of white marble. In this hall and the adjoining apartments were prepared tea, lemonade, &c., to which the company seated themselves. At this time the knights came in, and on their knee received their favors from their respective ladies. From these apartments they went up to a ball-room, decorated in a light, elegant style of painting and showing many festoons of flowers. The brilliancy of the whole was heightened by eighty-five mirrors decked with ribbons and flowers, and in the intermediate spaces were thirty-four branches. On the same floor were four drawing-rooms, with sideboards of refreshments, decorated and lighted in the style of the ball-room. The ball was opened by the knights and their ladies; and the dances continued till ten o'clock, when the windows were thrown open, and a magnificent bouquet of rockets began the fireworks. These were planned by Captain Montresor, the chief engineer, and consisted of twenty different displays, in great variety and beauty, and changing General Howe's arch into a variety of shapes and devices. At twelve o'clock (midnight) supper was announced, and large folding-doors, before concealed, sprung open, and discovered a magnificent saloon of two hundred and ten feet by forty feet, and twenty-two feet in height, with three alcoves on each side which served for sideboards. The sides were painted with vine-leaves and festoon-flowers, and fifty-six large pier-glasses, ornamented with green silk, artificial flowers, and ribbons. There were also one hundred branches trimmed, and eighteen lustres of twenty-four lights hung from the ceiling. There were three hundred wax tapers on the supper-tables, four hundred and thirty covers, and twelve hundred dishes. There were twenty-four black slaves in Oriental dresses, with silver collars and bracelets. Toward the close of the banquet, the herald with his trumpeters entered and announced the king and royal family's health, with other toasts. Each toast was followed by a flourish of music. After the supper, the company returned to the ball-room, and continued to dance until four o'clock in the morning.

"I omit to describe the two arches; but they were greatly embellished: they had two fronts in the Tuscan order. The pediment of one was adorned with naval trophies, and the other with military ones.

"Major André, who wrote a description of it (although his name is concealed), calls it 'the most splendid entertainment ever given by an army to its general.' The whole expense was borne by twenty-two field-officers. The managers were Sir John Wrotlesby, Colonel O'Hara, and Majors Gardiner and Montresor. This splendid pageant blazed out in one short night. Next day the enchantment was dissolved; and in exactly one month all these knights and the whole army chose to make their march from the city of Philadelphia."   WATSON.

Note 11. Page 225.

There rose a tumult wild without.

"While the British were indulging in the festivities of the night of the Meschianza, below the city, McLane was busy with a stratagem to break them up. He had one hundred infantry, in four squads, supported by Clow's dragoons. At ten at night they had reached the abatis in front of their redoubts, extending from the Schuylkill to the Globe Mill. These divisions carried camp-kettles filled with combustibles, with which at the proper signal they fired the whole line of abatis. The British beat the long roll, and their alarm-guns were fired from river to river, and were answered from the Park, in Southwark. The ladies, however, were so managed by the officers as to have taken the cannonade for any thing but the fact, and therefore continued the sports of the night. But the officers in charge on the lines understood the nature of the assailants, and gave pursuit and assault. He retired to the hills and fastnesses of the Wissahickon. After daylight, the British horse were in full force to pursue him, and finally took his picket and ensign at Barren Hill. McLane was afterwards attacked, and swam his horse across the Schuylkill, when some of Morgan's riflemen appeared to his protection. He then turned upon his pursuers, driving them in turn into their lines near the city." WATSON.

Note 12. Page 252.

Giving his daughter Berkley Hall,
And his blessing with the broad estate.

As some may not be aware of the baronial style in which certain of the early settlers of our country lived, and fearing that the description of "Berkley Hall" might be thought overdrawn, the author again avails himself of the invaluable "Annals" of Watson to select a couple of passages:—

"The Wharton Mansion, in Southwark, fronting the river, back from the present Navy-Yard, was a country-house of grandeur in its day. It was of large dimensions, with its lawns and trees; and, as a superior house, was chosen by the British officers of Howe's army for the celebration of the Meschianza. Wilton, the place once of Joseph Turner, down in the Neck, was the nonpareil of its day. It was the fashionable resort for genteel strangers. Every possible attention was paid to embellishment, and the garden-cultivation was superior. The grounds had ornamented clumps and ranges of trees. Many statues of fine marble (sold from a Spanish prize) were distributed through the grounds and avenues. The mansion-house and out-houses, still standing, show in some degree their former grandeur. The ceilings are high and covered with stucco-work, and the halls are large."

"*Duché's House.*—This was one of the most venerable-looking, antiquated houses of our city, built in 1758 for Parson Duché, the pastor of St. Peter's Church, as a gift from his father. It was taken down a few years ago. It was said to have been built after the pattern of one of the wings of Lambeth Palace. When first erected, it was considered quite out of town (corner of Third and Pine Streets), and for some time rested in lonely grandeur. It afterwards became the residence of Governor McKean; and, when we saw it as a boy, we derived from its contemplation conceptions of the state and dignity of a Governor which no subsequent structures could generate. It seemed the appropriate residence of some notable public man."

Note 13. Page 257.

Brave Percy, when his charger stood
First on the field of Brandywine.

"Among the gayest of the gay, as a volunteer in the suite of one of the British generals,—as tradition informs us,—was a sprightly and chivalrous descendant of the Percys. He was a noble and generous youth, and had volunteered on the present occasion as an amateur, to see how fields were won. As the young Percy came over the brow of the hill, he was observed suddenly to curb in his impatient steed; and the gay smile upon his lively features, changing at first to gravity, soon became sad and pensive as he glanced his bright eye over the extensive rolling landscape, now rife with animation. The wide prospect of gentle hill and dale, with forest and farm-house, the bright waters of the Brandywine, just appearing in one little winding section, in a low and beautiful valley on the right, formed of itself a picturesque view for the lover of the simple garniture of nature: all combined to make up a scene which it would hardly be supposed would have damped the ardor or clouded with gloom the fine features of a young officer whose proud lip would at any other moment have curled with scorn and his eye kindled with indignation at the remotest intimation of a want of firmness in the hour of trial. Yet, with a subdued and half-saddened eye, the young Percy, who but a moment before was panting to play the hero in the contest, paused for a moment longer. Then, calling his servant to his side, and taking his diamond-studded repeater from his pocket,—'Here,' said he, 'take this and deliver it to my sister in Northumberland. I have seen this field and this landscape before, in a dream in England. Here I shall fall. And'—drawing a heavy purse of gold from his pocket—' take this for yourself.' Saying this, he dashed forward with his fellows. The most obstinate fighting during the engagement took place near the centre, which rested upon the little stone meeting-house of the Quakers, and in the graveyard, walled on all sides by a thick stone masonwork, which, with the church, are yet standing as firmly as at the period of which we are writing. This enclosure was long and resolutely defended by the Americans; and it was near this place, about the middle of the action, that the noble young Percy fell, as he believed he had been doomed to do. The enclosure was at length scaled, and carried by the bayonet. The wounded were taken into the meeting-house, built by peacemakers for the worship of the God of peace, though now the centre of the bloody strife; and the dead were inhumed in one corner of the burying-ground in which they had many of them been slain. Just before our visit, a grave had been dug, and the remains of a British soldier disinterred. A part of his shoes remained: a few pieces of red cloth, a button likewise, marked '44th Reg^t.', and a flattened bullet,—probably the winged messenger of death to the wearer,—were also found; both of which were given to us by the good man near by the meeting-house."   WATSON.

THE END.

STEREOTYPED BY L. JOHNSON & CO.
PHILADELPHIA.